A revelation

The night was insane. He must be high on adrenaline. The game had been incredible. The car was—face it, the car was unlike anything he'd ever planned on riding in during his life. And as designated driver, he was going to get to drive it home.

But really, he wasn't even thinking about that drive.

Because he couldn't get rid of the realization that had rocked and cracked his world like a broken windshield. Just before the car had pulled up.

She might be crazy—wearing that thin dress on a night that was maybe twenty-nine degrees. And she might be a nerd—because, really, who from Liberty High School ever applied to go to Stanford? And she was most definitely a walking disaster area.

But she was also *beautiful*.

OTHER BOOKS YOU MAY ENJOY

Academy 7	Anne Osterlund
Aurelia	Anne Osterlund
Exile	Anne Osterlund
Faithful	Janet Fox
The Fine Art of Truth or Dare	Melissa Jensen
If I Stay	Gayle Forman
Impossible	Nancy Werlin
Lock and Key	Sarah Dessen
Matched	Ally Condie
The Sky Is Everywhere	Jandy Nelson
Stay With Me	Paul Griffin
Try Not to Breathe	Jennifer Hubbard

Salvation

ANNE OSTERLUND

speak

An Imprint of Penguin Group (USA) Inc.

SPEAK

Published by the Penguin Group

Penguin Group (USA) Inc., 345 Hudson Street, New York, New York 10014, U.S.A.

Penguin Group (Canada), 90 Eglinton Avenue East, Suite 700, Toronto, Ontario, Canada M4P 2Y3
(a division of Pearson Penguin Canada Inc.)

Penguin Books Ltd, 80 Strand, London WC2R 0RL, England

Penguin Ireland, 25 St Stephen's Green, Dublin 2, Ireland (a division of Penguin Books Ltd)

Penguin Group (Australia), 250 Camberwell Road, Camberwell, Victoria 3124, Australia
(a division of Pearson Australia Group Pty Ltd)

Penguin Books India Pvt Ltd, 11 Community Centre,
Panchsheel Park, New Delhi – 110 017, India

Penguin Group (NZ), 67 Apollo Drive, Rosedale, Auckland 0632, New Zealand
(a division of Pearson New Zealand Ltd.)

Penguin Books (South Africa) (Pty) Ltd, 24 Sturdee Avenue,
Rosebank, Johannesburg 2196, South Africa

Penguin Books Ltd, Registered Offices: 80 Strand, London WC2R 0RL, England

Published by Speak, an imprint of Penguin Group (USA) Inc., 2013

10 9 8 7 6 5 4 3 2 1

Copyright © Anne Osterlund, 2013
All rights reserved

LIBRARY OF CONGRESS CATALOGING-IN-PUBLICATION DATA IS AVAILABLE
Speak 978-0-14-241770-6

Printed in the United States of America

For all the cast members of *The Tempest,*

Hamlet, Julius Caesar, Macbeth, and *The Taming of the Shrew.*

Burn spectacular.

Salvation

Prologue

SACRILEGE

"So you gonna ask her out?" came the inevitable question.

Salva groaned, though it was hard not to let his gaze linger a little too long on Char's bare shoulders, gleaming in the late August sun. She knew how to look sexy even at church. "Are you kidding me, man? I've known her since I was eight. We were practically raised together."

"Must have been rough chasin' *her* through your sprinkler." Pepe grinned, then leaned back against the outer brick wall and rolled a wrapper off a *limón* candy. "You want one?" he offered.

Salva shook his head. His father would blow a gasket if he caught him with it at mass. "Look, you want to date Char, she's all yours."

"Right. We both know she ain't lustin' after my rep," Pepe said.

Salva elbowed him, though jabbing his best friend in the chest was a lot like elbowing the statue of *El Pípila,* hard as stone. "You break a few more sacking records this fall, and she might start."

"Everybody knows you're gonna be the prime merchandise at school this year," said Pepe. "She didn't wear that outfit for me."

Once again Salva found himself staring at the teal-green top with the off-the-shoulder sleeves. There was no denying the fact that Charla looked *fine*.

His best friend might be right that she'd dressed on Salva's behalf, but that didn't mean Salva could ask her out. It wasn't just that he'd known her forever or that their parents were always pushing their children together; he'd dated Char back in their freshman year for two months, and despite the fact that they shared the same culture, their parents worked the same shift at the onion-processing plant, and he and Char had been in the same class since second-grade migrant summer school, they really didn't have much to say to each other.

"We have nothing in common," he tried to explain to Pepe.

That went over like a flat football. "Have you lost it, man? She's hot, and you're a friggin' god at our school. What more do you want?"

Salva shrugged. "Someone who wants the same things I do, I guess." He'd never heard Charla mention any grander ambition than making head cheerleader, which hadn't worked out, since her mom had refused to let Char join the squad.

"Like a state football title?" Pepe mocked. "Not a whole lotta girls lookin' for that."

Salva grinned. His best friend had pretty much a two-track mind: girls and football, in the reverse order. "Like college . . . and a future."

"Yeah, well, we can't all be gods and brainiacs, can we?" The linebacker reached out as though to slug him.

"Knock it off." Salva blocked Pepe's fist. "If my father thinks I'm being blasphemous in church, he just might yank me off the team. He already says it's too much time off from my studies."

"Has he seen your GPA?"

"Yes, but I have to get a scholarship. I can't just coast in on football."

"Hey!" Pepe argued. "I *am* taking geometry."

"Enjoy that. Lundell's mind-numbing."

"I'd rather be numb than dead. I heard AP calc is like an execution."

"I'll handle it."

The church bell started to ring, and Char chose that moment to stroll past both Pepe and Salva, her brown shoulders glimmering in the sunlight before disappearing into the vestibule. "Don't know what good all that brainpower is doing you, man," Pepe whispered, "if you can't even recognize a God-given gift like her."

1

COLLISION

"Salvador Resendez." The sharp tone came from inside the Pen—aka the school's ominous square front office with its bulletproof windows, legal-form wallpaper, and particleboard cubicles for dividing kids in trouble. Principal Markham appeared. His flabby arms crossed over his paunch as he leaned up against the wraparound counter that separated the office staff from the reality of Liberty High School. "It's about time. The welcome ceremony starts in five minutes."

Salva shrugged his shoulders. "Yeah, the girls are taking care of that. I'm doing activity sign-ups on Friday." He figured he ought to be able to relax and enjoy the first day of the school year.

Markham's uneven mustache dipped down at the corners. "You are the president of the Associated Student Body."

It's not my fault Julie Tri-Ang transferred to some fancy prep school. VP would have looked plenty good on a college application.

Salva started toward the gym, braving the last-minute traffic of sprinting achievers and dawdling slackers, but Markham called after him. "I need you back here before you go to class."

"Why?"

"Later, Resendez. Now move."

The assembly lasted twenty minutes. Nalani Villetti, who'd been elected secretary and was now vice president, at least did her job introducing the teachers and staff members, but Kaitlyn, who had left her speech at home, panicked in front of the crowd. Salva ended up having to vamp and do the whole "Welcome back, everybody. We're going to have an awesome year" bit. Not that giving the speech was a big deal. It just wasn't the low-key start he'd intended for his senior year.

Neither was visiting the principal's office.

"Come in, Salvador," Markham said, dropping his thick body into the padded chair behind his desk. "Seems we have a problem with your current class schedule."

Do I have to go through this again? Salva braced his hands against the doorframe. Just because he had taken a few classes ahead of the curve didn't mean he should have to fight for the advanced courses every year. Why did they always try to schedule students into a box?

"You aren't signed up for an English class," Markham said, the joints on his chair squealing as he leaned back his torso.

Salva let out a breath. Was that all? "I took senior English last year, remember? I started freshman lit as an eighth grader.

5

You're the one who made me do that." Well, technically, it had been Mrs. Lukowski, his middle-school English teacher, who had strong-armed the high school into accepting him and four other top students. Back then, Salva had been a bit afraid of Mrs. Lukowski.

"You still need four years of English in high school. It's state law."

Salva just stared. This was stupid, far too stupid for him to waste his breath explaining why. "You're saying I need to retake freshman English in high school to get it to count?"

"Don't be obtuse." Markham wrapped his thick fingers around an insulated coffee mug. "You need to take AP English."

Salva's grip on the doorframe faltered. "With the Mercenary?"

Markham grimaced, looked as though he might rebut the use of the school-wide moniker, then disdained the effort and took a swig from his mug. Coffee drizzled around the edge of his mouth and dripped down onto the mountain of papers piled on his cheap metal desk. "You're more than capable of taking her course."

Capable. Not stupid. "I have advanced physics and AP calc. You can't expect me to take on the Mercenary, too."

The principal gave him a look of false pity, then lifted a coffee-stained printout from the top of his pile. "Your new schedule. I removed you from phys ed II. A waste of your time, Mr. Resendez."

Salva fumed. He knew better than Markham what was a waste of his own time.

"That's all." The principal tossed the printout across the desk and gulped another swig of coffee. "Hurry, or you'll be tardy for second period."

That would be AP English. Great.

Salva snagged the revised schedule, then freed himself from the Pen and made a beeline for his locker. By the time he'd retrieved his notebook, the hall had cleared. He allowed himself to lengthen his strides and pick up speed. The walls flashed past, a blur of peeled paint and dented steel. He swept around the corner—

And ran headlong into the walking disaster area.

Beth could have killed him. All the time he spent oblivious to her and he chose *this* moment to intersect her path. She was already late, and she'd been trying desperately to unwrap her remaining school supplies so that the second-period teacher wouldn't glare at her the way the homeroom instructor had. Papers flew out of Beth's arms, across the floor, and under the slice of space beneath the lockers. Her open backpack fell, emptying its contents into the pile. Devastation.

She dropped to her knees.

He had the audacity to sigh. As if ramming his way around the corner was her fault. Frantically, she started to scramble, cramming pencils, folders, notebooks, erasers, and books into her backpack.

The bell rang.

She reached for a binder, and his hand stopped her.

He pulled the object toward him and snapped open the rings. "You know," he said, "if you put the paper in here, it won't make such a mess."

She glared at his slicked hair and spotless T-shirt. Why did organized people act so patronizing? But it was hard to argue with him when she realized he'd picked up every stray piece of lined paper. "We're late," she muttered as her only form of revenge.

In the nine years she'd known him, she couldn't remember *El Perfecto* ever being tardy.

He just nodded, handing back the filled binder, then stood, straightened his shoulders, and walked into AP English.

Salva scanned the stark classroom. The seniors sat so frozen in their seats you'd have thought the air-conditioning was working. Every chair at the back of the room was already filled. With nerds.

Luka was in the front row. Salva liked Luka. If it weren't for his phenomenal speed as a running back, nobody at Liberty High would be headed for the state football championship. But sometimes the white guy was just strange.

What sane person would sit in the front row before the Mercenary? Her scowling expression curled Salva's stomach. The pointed toe of her shoe tapped out a funeral dirge, and she wielded a bright red marker as if she might stab him with it.

Salva cut his losses and sat down behind Luka.

The walking disaster area came in next. But she didn't know when to hide. Instead, she stood there, stuttering her apologies, trying to untangle the strap of her backpack from her frizzy brown hair, and dropping things, first her pencil, then an eraser, while the entire class waited for her to just sit down.

"What are you doing here, man?" Luka whispered to Salva.

Markham, Salva mouthed. Enough said.

Luka rolled his eyes in response.

What are *you* doing here? Salva wanted to ask, but a second glance around the room revealed the presence of Nalani Villetti, the girl whom Luka had been following around like a puppy for the past six months. Sooner or later, he'd wake up to the fact that she was letting him follow her.

But Salva didn't have time to clarify that point just now.

The Mercenary had headed his way with a stapled form that was already in everyone else's possession. Her hand slammed down on his desk, leaving a synopsis of the three million hours of work she expected this quarter. "Welcome to AP English," she told the class.

Yeah, friggin' welcome.

Somehow Salva made it through the rest of that torture session. He cruised through finance and survived the first-day lecture for AP calc. Mostly due to the promise of lunch.

He conquered the food line by piling his tray with as much protein as he could and snatching an extra milk, then touched down on the prime spot in the cafeteria, Table Numero Uno, bequeathed to him by last year's seniors and now solely the possession of Salva and his friends.

"What the H, man? I thought you were takin' PE. You know I had to run relay with Tosa here?" Pepe elbowed Ricardo Tosa, whom Salva liked almost as much as his best friend. Tosa was *huge*. Maybe six-three. Despite his extra height, he mostly just warmed the bench, but his goofy, lighthearted personality was the heart of the football team. Everybody loved him. Even Pepe, who was all about the win.

"D'you lose?" Salva asked, sitting down on the bench beside his best friend.

"No, of course not," Pepe replied. "The class is mostly just sophomores. I had to talk Gregson into letting us in, you know. I thought you were comin' with."

"Markham," Salva said.

Pepe just stared, French fries in his hand. Not as quick on the uptake as Luka.

"He stuck me in AP English," Salva explained.

The fries dropped to the table.

Tosa picked them up, dipped them in Tabasco, and swallowed them before his friend had recovered.

"You aren't serious," Pepe said.

"As a playoff game," replied Salva.

"F-it. Tell Markham to go for a dunk. I bet he never took an AP course in his life. You don't wind up in a sinkhole like this with a high-powered degree."

Pepe had a point, but it wouldn't do any good to go on hating Markham. It was a little late to undo the decision to take freshman lit in the eighth grade. Salva explained the logistics.

"You see." Tosa grinned. "It pays to be an underachiever."

No way. Salva's gut rebelled against the statement. The cost for that mind-set was *far* too steep. He glanced around the sunken cafeteria. Salva knew the life story of probably 90 percent of the kids filling the room. Despite the open campus, almost the entire student body was here for free and reduced lunch. The one thing that made you stick out at Liberty High like nothing else was money. No one had it.

If they did, they switched to somewhere out of the district, like Julie Tri-Ang. Not that Julie really had money. She just had the grades for a prep-school scholarship. And a set of parents who weren't afraid to have their daughter board two hundred miles away.

Salva wasn't interested in switching schools. He had friends here. And only one year left to spend with them. But he wasn't hanging around afterward to run a gas pump. He'd seen plenty of guys who did that, and most of them ended up in prison for dealing.

"Luka was there," Salva said, as if to validate his own part in the travesty that was AP lit.

"He would be," Pepe groaned.

Tosa stole another handful of fries.

"Luka's all right," Salva said.

"Yeah, I guess." Pepe shrugged.

11

"You're just jealous 'cause he's the only guy in this school who dominates a football field more than you."

"What's that supposed to mean, *quarterback*?"

Salva dismissed the comment. He had a good head on his shoulders—could choose a play and run it. Strong enough for Liberty, but he wasn't of the same caliber as the guys who played his position in college. And in truth, he didn't want to be. He didn't want to be crushed three million times before he got out of his twenties.

"Nalani Villetti was there, too."

"Mmm-hmm." Pepe had clearly lost interest, his eyes on something else. "Don't look now, but guess who's headed our way."

Salva didn't have to guess. He could tell by the heat in Pepe's voice that Char was coming. And she wasn't wearing a turtleneck.

She wasn't alone either.

"Hey, gorgeous," Tosa greeted the long-legged blonde at Char's side. He grinned as if he was joking, but no one was fooled.

"Hi, sweetheart." Linette flipped her golden hair over one shoulder, propped herself on the outside of the bench, and leaned her hip against Tosa's waist. Whether or not *she* was joking was harder to tell.

Char, whose tight shirt and tighter jeans battled with the dress code, stood waiting next to Salva, despite the fact that there was no space beside him on the bench.

He hated that—how she'd just stand there waiting for him to read her mind whenever she wanted something.

Pepe moved over, and Salva reminded himself to give his best friend a lecture on loyalty. Char slid in between them.

"Listen, guys." Linette set her chin on Tosa's shoulder. "My parents are water-skiing this weekend. You wanna come over while they're gone for a little back-to-school action?" She popped her tropical-orange lips. "Saturday 'bout two?"

"I'm working," Salva said. Scut every weekend at the onion-processing plant. His father's idea.

"Ah, man!" Pepe frowned. "You're not serious."

Salva shrugged. Sorting onions wasn't his view of a career path, but whatever. His older brother and sister had done their part to pay his way, so Salva owed it to his two younger sisters to do the same. Plus, he could work around his football schedule.

"Can't you talk your way out of it?" Linette asked.

Char's fingers brushed his arm.

"No," he replied.

The fingers retreated, slightly.

"Well, I'm in," Pepe stated.

Tosa laughed. "Oh, we knew *you* wouldn't give up your Saturday for cash." Of all of them, Pepe was the most flush. Not that his mom had money. Ms. Hart, who had ditched her husband's last name of Real after he'd split when her son was twelve, had raised Pepe on a middle-school secretary's salary. But his grandparents spoiled him rotten.

"And you, Ricardo?" Linette eased her long leg inside the bench so her right knee fell in front of Tosa and her left one rested behind. "Are you coming?"

Like that was gonna get a no.

"Prob'ly." Tosa turned as orange as his polished-off Tabasco. "I'll have to ask at the machine shop, but the boss owes me hours."

"Good." She slid back.

"Aren't you *chicas* eating?" asked Tosa as he bit into his well-doctored burger. Juice from the tomatoes ran down his chin.

Both girls dismissed his question. Always dieting, one of the things that had driven Salva crazy when he was dating Char. What were you supposed to do with a girlfriend who wouldn't eat?

"So *you're* coming this weekend, aren't you, Char?" Pepe prodded.

"I'm not sure," she replied.

"What?!" he reacted as if the sagging ceiling had fallen in. "The worth-it factor goes down by half if you're not there."

Char lowered her eyes. She'd used glitter eye shadow, not much, but still a little creepy. "My mother would have to give permission."

That's not gonna happen. Char's mother was the *queen* of overprotection. No cheerleading. No R-rated movies. No overnight field trips. Nothing that would leave her daughter exposed to the hazards of, well, a guy like Pepe.

"I thought maybe if I could tell her someone would be there"—Char raised the sparkling eyelids to look straight at Salva—"someone she trusts . . ."

Right. She wanted his name for an alibi. He'd been playing her chaperone since they were kids. She could ride the bus to summer school *if* he rode with her. She could go to the music concert *if* he was also going. She could attend the dance *if* he escorted her.

Pepe wheedled, "Come on, man, if you can't come, that's cool; but you're not gonna leave her sittin' home, are you? Just because you're makin' love to some onions."

And you're gonna take over as chaperone, huh? Salva felt a twinge prick his conscience. Charla *was* a little like a sister to him—he had known her so long. He wouldn't have advised one of his real sisters to date Pepe.

Char leaned closer, her arm against Salva's, her knee pressing his. There was nothing *sisterly* in that gaze.

So much for his conscience.

"All right," Salva said, "use my name."

2

A GRAVEYARD BUTTERFLY

Beth savored the silence of the emptied-out school hallway that afternoon and devoured the final pages of *Wuthering Heights*. She could no longer feel the oppressive late summer heat or the hard metal of the locker at her back. Gone were the crumpled papers, broken pencils, and discarded candy wrappers on the tiled floor. She was on the cold English moors with the wind blowing around her and the whistle of death in the air.

A trio of voices suddenly invaded the end of the hall. Beth rushed through the last page. A banging locker emphasized the drama of the final line, and she looked up, just in time to see *El Perfecto* sprinting past, no doubt in a rush to get to football practice. Apparently, tardiness was a new thing for him.

Nalani came up at a much more relaxed pace, her pink canvas book bag slung over one shoulder.

"So what was the meeting about?" Beth asked her best friend.

"Who knows?" Nalani's eyes shone as she rolled them.

She glanced over her shoulder, then lowered her voice. "Just Markham on a power trip. I'll tell you on the walk home."

Beth stuffed *Wuthering Heights* back into her locker, not wanting to lose the book again and owe a fine to the library as she had back in June. Then she gathered her supplies and hefted her backpack.

Nalani was already halfway to the back exit, which led, naturally, to the football field. Beth hurried after her.

The team had stretched out in lines, five rows of testosterone-filled tight pants and loose jerseys hopping up and down in jumping jacks. The compact blond with the number 12 plastered on his front wasted no time sending Nalani a wave, even though he was leading the entire team—minus *El Perfecto,* who must not have made it out of the locker room yet—in the warm-ups. The team mimicked the wave.

Nalani pretended not to notice.

Which was fine because Beth didn't want to hear the one-sided conversation about all the things Luka had done that day.

Heat radiated off the black asphalt path as the girls curved their way along the field, back toward the front of the building. Beth realized she had forgotten her sunscreen, but it didn't matter much. Far too late to worry about freckles. By August, she was always a mess.

The three thousand pounds of football players, now jogging in place, disappeared behind her.

"Okay, we're outside," she said. "Now, what was your surprise ASB meeting about?"

Nalani groaned. "Markham wanted to go over all the responsibilities of our new positions. He said Salva has to do the announcements at the assemblies. I only fill in when he's gone. Kaitlyn has to take the notes. We have to elect a new parliamentarian to fill her old spot. Which is all fine, of course, except Salva didn't want to be there because he was anxious to get to practice. He and Markham got into an argument about who should be able to schedule meetings and how it's not fair to hold them without advance notice. Of course, Markham just blew him off."

Beth tried to fix the uneven shoulder straps on her backpack as she listened.

"It's a good thing I have such an excellent best friend who's willing to wait," Nalani added, smiling at her.

Beth smiled back.

Her best friend kept talking. "But I mean, really, what did Markham expect? It isn't like he didn't know Salva is booked after school in the fall; but *oh*, no one else could become president. I mean Salva didn't want the job. I don't see why Markham wouldn't even discuss the idea of me taking Julie's spot."

The slide toggles on Beth's backpack straps refused to adjust. "Did you want it?"

Nalani shrugged.

"I'm sorry, Ni," Beth said softly, trying to protect her best friend's feelings. "But maybe this is a good thing. You're already so busy . . ." What Beth didn't say was that Nalani had a habit of volunteering for too much and only following through on about half of it.

"Well, we could have discussed it." Nalani took the backpack away from Beth, smoothed out the puckers on each of the straps, and corrected the length. The two girls turned the corner, taking a route that led first to Nalani's, then to Beth's. Ni returned the pack, raising her voice over a barking hound dog and a whining air conditioner. "It just doesn't seem fair that Markham thinks Salva is the only one who can do the job."

Beth nodded in sympathy, though the principal had a point. After all, if Salva had decided to run for president in the first place, no one doubted he would have won.

Ni climbed onto the curb. "I mean, he's not perfect."

Beth's head shot up at that, and a warm blush spread over her cheeks before she could control it.

Her best friend must have noticed. "Sorry . . ." Ni trailed off.

Was Beth never going to escape the repercussions of one silly junior-high crush? *Everyone has had a crush on him. It's not like I own the embarrassment.* She cringed to think of herself in the eighth grade: naïve, suffering from the bombardment of braces, two bouts of head lice, and the illusion that Salvador Resendez would one day magically look across the freshman-lit classroom and realize that she, Beth, was perfect for him.

"There's nothing—" Beth tried to say, but her friend ended the discussion.

"We won't talk about him."

It wasn't him, Beth told herself. *It was just an image. Middle schoolers fall in love with image all the time.* Though she couldn't quite push away the image of him today, picking up all her papers before he went on to class.

"Well, I guess I'll see you tomorrow," Nalani said.

Beth startled, having failed to realize they had reached the plastic fence around her best friend's lawn.

"Unless you want to come in for dinner," Ni added.

"No . . . thank you." Beth looked up at the freshly painted house with the barrage of sunflower stickies in the window. Better to save her invitations for when she needed them.

Besides, she wanted to talk to her grandmother.

Nalani gave her friend a quick shoulder squeeze, then traipsed through the arched garden trellis, pausing to adjust the hose caught on the back of the stone deer decorating the path.

Beth fled, not wanting to regret her choice to turn down supper.

She smiled as she reached the graveyard. "Morbid," her mother would have said about her daughter's desire to visit the cemetery, but Beth kicked off her sandals and waded through the fresh-cut grass. The cool strands tickled her ankles, and the sweet scent of late roses clung to the air. Pale yellow, blue, and pink tombstones scattered the green in a pastel palate.

A squirrel rushed across the grass and scurried up an old oak tree, the fluffy gray tail disappearing among the branches. Beth approached, watching to see if it would emerge again, but when it did not, she swung off her backpack and slid to the ground beneath the tree's outstretched shadow. And beside the slender pink stone with the name GLORIA MAY COURANT etched in the center.

"Hello, Grandma," said Beth. "I'm sorry I'm late." She explained about Nalani's meeting. "You know she always has something happening. I'm sure you aren't surprised." It felt right to be here. Grandma had always expected Beth to share about the first day of school, a ritual that Beth hadn't wanted to stop now.

"It was a pretty good day," Beth went on, "for the first, you know. I'm not sure I'll survive trigonometry; but I thought the same thing about algebra II, and it turned out all right. All the answers are still in the back of the book, so I'll know when to ask Nalani for help." She knew Grandma would remind her that Beth's final math scores had outpaced Ni's all the way through school. But grades, and confidence in math, were two different things.

A robin hopped down onto the grass about twenty feet from the pink tombstone. Beth stopped talking so that she wouldn't frighten him. He pecked his way closer, hopping four or five inches at a time and up onto the mound of turned earth. The grass there had not quite grown in yet. The robin preened, raising his chest and showing off, then disappeared in a sudden rush of wings.

Beth's head swam with the questions her grandmother had always asked. *Do you like your teachers? Did you make any new friends? Were you on* time *for everything?*

Obediently, Beth answered the questions, though she skimmed through her problems with being late. She told herself the aversion had nothing to do with crashing into Salva Resendez, though Grandma would have wanted to hear about him so she could repeat the story, for the hundredth time, about how she had dropped her cupcake during her granddaughter's third-grade Valentine's Day party, and Salva had given her his.

The sun continued to shine as Beth talked. And talked and talked, letting her tongue flow as easily as her pencil when inspiration struck. She kept talking even when her throat grew dry and she had to clear it every few seconds. But then her stomach began to growl, and she realized it must be dinnertime. She'd forgotten her watch, of course. It seemed silly to wear a watch in a building where every room had a clock timed down to the exact second.

Reluctantly, Beth reached for her backpack. "I should probably go. I'm on my own for supper tonight. Mom's taking classes after work and attending meetings."

Grandma would be happy with that, though she wouldn't have said. She didn't like to encourage false hope. Still, she would want to know.

"Love you ever." Beth stood, then wound her way once around the oak tree, her eyes peering up to check for the long-lost squirrel. No tail flashed so she turned her attention down, slid back into her sandals, and headed for home.

The weeds had grown clear up to the trailer. She should mow them, but it seemed a waste now that no one stayed here during the day; and soon it would be fall, the season defined by nature's refuse. She picked her way along the path of flattened cheatgrass and tugged on the screen door.

It stuck. She rattled the latch and jerked harder, until the door swung free with a bang.

The trailer smelled of sour milk from cereal bowls. Beth sighed, letting her backpack obey gravity, then she stepped from the worn carpet on the right half of the room and crossed to the peeling linoleum on the left.

The sink was disgusting. She forced herself to reach into the scum-covered water to retrieve a frying pan and wooden spoon, then turned over the dishpan and watched the cold liquid disappear down the drain. Beth flipped on the faucet, letting it run while the hot water decided whether to work.

She detoured to the fridge and yanked open the freezer, too fast because a paper slid off the door. Eagerly, she reached into the open Popsicle box. One left. She grinned and tugged out the treat.

The clear wrapper peeled away, and she tossed it into the garbage can, along with the box.

Back to the sink to test the water. *Hot.* She slid the dishpan under the faucet, poured in the soap, then tasted the Popsicle. It was red, the flavor a bit like children's medicine, but at least the treat was cold.

Suds in the dishpan threatened the rim, and she turned off the water, then caught sight again of the fridge. And frowned. Her eyes swooped to the floor, where they spotted the fallen paper sticking out from beneath the stove. Quickly she scooped up the sheet, held it straight against the freezer door so the paper would be easy for her mother to read, then secured the Alcoholics Anonymous pledge with a bright pink-and-green butterfly magnet, Grandma's favorite.

AND A GENTLEMAN

The hot evening air blasted Salva in the face as he swung out of the school's main doors and stepped into the parking lot. His chest felt numb and his arms and legs like they had been drained. That happened after ten extra laps.

Dios, ayúdame.

Salva's father was in the parking lot. There was no mistaking that battered green pickup with its strips of duct tape along the lower half of the cab.

His father's words rang out the open window. "You are late."

Salva let his head fall back and his eyes rest on the still brilliant blue sky. *Would this day never end?*

He hauled his backpack and sweaty football clothes across the lot and up to the driver's side door, then waited for the inevitable question of why he was the only football player still here.

It didn't come.

He peered into the cab and saw the reason. Señora Mendoza, her hair up in a scarf, her lunch box on the dash, sat beside the passenger door. His father and Char's mother must have come straight from work—Salva checked his watch—which meant they had been waiting together for half an hour.

"I'm sorry." He didn't bother to point out that he hadn't known they were coming or to explain that the reason he was late was because Coach Robson and Markham didn't see eye to eye on when it was important for Salva to be at practice. *Papá* would have sided with the principal.

Señor Resendez descended from the cab for his son to enter.

Salva deposited his stuff in the pickup bed, careful to avoid the patches of grease, then climbed into the cab and greeted Señora Mendoza, whose response was terribly polite for a woman who had spent an extra thirty minutes in a pickup after a twelve-hour shift. She worked under his father, so her schedule was subject to his. And Señor Resendez, despite—or maybe because of—being manager, always accepted the longest hours.

"*¿Cómo fue tu primer día?*" *Papá* asked about his son's day.

Salva shrugged. As first days went, it had pretty much sucked. No phys ed. AP English. Markham's surprise meeting, for no reason.

Salva's father didn't need to know any of this.

"You have homework?" came the next question as Señor Resendez steered out of the parking lot.

Twenty pages of *Paradise Lost* to read for the Mercenary, but *Papá* didn't need to know that either. "It was only the first day," Salva replied.

He expected a complaint about how every school day should be used to the fullest, but the actual response was a surprise. *"Bueno."* Señor Resendez grinned over his son's head. "Señora Mendoza and I think you should teach Charla to drive."

¿Qué?

"You have time tonight. Is still light for more hours."

No, no, no, no, no. His father knew Char didn't have a license. She wasn't legal, unlike her younger brother, and she couldn't get a permit without documentation, so it hadn't been safe for her to take driver's ed. *Though, of course, that's why she needs the lesson.* Salva needed a reason to refuse that his father might actually accept. *"Mira,* this pickup *es imposible."* Salva pointed at the wires springing from the dead stereo and at the open glovebox door that refused to shut. "You can't expect her to learn to drive in this . . ." *Hunk of junk.*

As if to prove the point, the vehicle chose that moment to stop in the middle of the road and jerk up and down before returning to forward motion. His father relaxed the gas pedal and crawled past cop corner at about fifteen miles per hour.

"You see, *Papá.* It barely obeys you."

A decent argument. One that might have worked with someone else, but his father had an ulterior motive. "You are intelligent, *hijo.* You can help her."

Salva was not so sure. He hadn't managed to help Char learn her multiplication tables or memorize the names of all the countries in Europe. And he certainly hadn't been able to help her pass the state's high-school standardized test.

"But *Papá*"—this time the protest was weak—"where would we practice?"

His father sobered. "Take to her to the Fentzsen place. Mr. Fentzsen no will mind."

Salva felt his chest go cold. He hadn't been to the Fentzsen farm since *Mamá*'s death four years ago.

The pickup shuddered to a halt outside the Mendoza home, and Salva and his father bailed from the vehicle so that Char's mother could climb out. The door on the passenger side hadn't worked for years. She exited, then hurried inside to suggest the idea of the driving lesson to her daughter.

What were the chances Char would turn it down? Though she had never liked studying with Salva, even when they were dating. Maybe she wouldn't care for this either.

But the brief grasp at hope departed as Char emerged from the front door. Her hairstyle had changed since lunch, the ebony strands tied back instead of sculpted with spray, and she had exchanged her too-tight jeans for a pair of very white, very short shorts.

His father greeted her with a huge smile and a joke in Spanish that she didn't seem to get. Char's mastery of Spanish was worse than her English. Then *Papá* gave her a hand up into the pickup. "You two go," he said. "I can walk home from here." Then he squeezed his son's shoulder and admonished, "Be a gentleman."

Battle lost, Salva accepted the keys and climbed up next to Char. She had seated herself in the middle, instead of sliding over to the window, despite the fact that the rip in the center section of the seat must have scratched her bare thighs.

He turned the key, pushed the gas pedal, and felt the engine die. *Oh, this was going to be great.* "Sorry," he said as he revved the engine for the second time and felt the pedal catch. "Hope this doesn't mess with your plans."

She didn't reply.

Of course not. This was Char. *Nothing to say to each other.* It had been like this their whole dating experience. Why would she want to relive that?

"So . . . how was your day?" he asked in a pathetic attempt at conversation.

She just shrugged, her hand dropping to the seat. Alongside his thigh.

They headed through town, her body inching closer to his every time the pickup chose to stop and jerk.

He tried again. "What classes are you taking?"

"Study hall." Then the volume of her voice sank. "R. English, R. writing, R. math." The *R* stood for remedial. There were no options on the remedial track. The topic died.

Silence. He tried to focus on the road. Houses faded in the

rearview mirror, and the fields engulfed him, the strong scent of dust and sweet onions assailing his nostrils. Then memory invaded—his mother at the head of the harvest crew: her long black braid swinging, her straw hat shading her face, her laughter chiming with the voices of the other workers, her shouts of command to the truck drivers, her strong grip as she showed Salva how to top onions, her complete and total exhaustion after a day in these same fields.

The pickup stopped again, jerking him out of his memories. He'd missed a turn. Salva swerved up on the bank and brought the vehicle around.

Char clutched the dash. "Is something wrong?"

Now she talks. He backtracked a hundred yards, then curved the vehicle onto a straight stretch of emptiness. The gravel beneath the wheels was thin, and the dirt blew up like powder.

Salva pulled over to the side of the road. "Okay, this is the clutch. This is the gear shift. The gears go in a pattern, but the picture has rubbed off so you'll have to remember the locations." He rattled on for about a minute before he realized he was talking for himself. Char had never learned well by listening.

Get a grip. He ran his hand through his hair, then swung open the door and hopped out of the pickup. "So we'd better switch places."

She slid into the driver's seat, not getting out, which meant he had to climb back in over her. *Be a gentleman,* his father's advice rang in his mind.

Sí, Papá, but what do you do when she's not a lady?

Salva talked Char through the use of the mirrors, only one of which was still adjustable, then explained how to start the pickup. "Don't worry if the engine doesn't catch the first time. It doesn't a lot. Just listen and feel the vibration beneath your foot; the feel should change when it works. Then you can let up on the clutch."

She tried.

Nothing happened.

She tried five more times. Each time, the engine revved, then died when she lifted her foot.

On her seventh try, the whole pickup shook like Mount St. Helens, then died again.

Her eyes had widened, and the color had drained from her face, the same look she had always had right before fleeing the homework table.

"Look." Salva lowered his voice. "You don't have to do this. We could just drive around and tell them I gave you a lesson."

"No," she said, soft but serious. "I won't end up like my mother."

He wrinkled his brow.

"I won't be like her," Char insisted, "having to count on someone else to take her to work, stuck in a nothing job because Renaldo's father brought her here and then abandoned her without a visa, scared all the time that he will come back and want Renaldo and she won't have any power because she's not a citizen. And too scared to try to become one because she might risk what little she has here."

Salva stared, not sure he'd ever heard Char say so much at one time in his life. Of course, she was right. Unless she could drive, she would be trapped.

"Okay," he said, "how about if I start the pickup, and you work on the steering?"

Relief flooded her eyes.

He maneuvered over her again, revved the engine, and shifted into first, then second. He couldn't slide back to the center of the seat without causing a wreck, so he wedged himself by the driver's door, trying not to lean on it because it had been known to fly open.

He didn't have much time to think about that, though, because Char had taken over the gas pedal with her own foot. The pickup roared, then almost died, but eventually took off in a long wobbly line. Her fingers clutched the steering wheel so hard, her knuckles shone white.

The vehicle reached a fork. "Take the left," he said. "It curves, so try to stay on the right side of the road, just in case someone might be coming."

She bit her lip and nodded.

They started off around the corner.

The wind picked up and blew a tumbleweed across the gravel.

She gasped, and her hands vibrated.

"It's okay," he said. "It's just—"

A pheasant. The bird burst from the stubble right in front of the tires.

Char cried out and jerked the steering wheel to the right. The pickup rocked up on the bank, then swerved back, skidding and heading straight for the ditch.

"Watch out!" Salva shouted.

And she dropped both hands from the wheel. "Just take it. Take it!"

He jammed his feet underneath hers, grabbed the wheel, and held his body up with his grip as the driver's-side door swung open.

Char's panicked scream ripped through Salva's eardrums.

Though he was the one in danger, hanging on to the wheel and blocking her from the open door. He pushed on the brake, felt the vehicle thrust forward, fighting his command, then finally stagger to a halt.

Char was still screaming.

Salva's chest heaved, his heart thundering above his rib cage. He didn't care what his father said. Someone else could give her lessons.

4

D. Salva slumped down in his chair and stared at the letter printed at the top of his essay with a felt-tip marker. In green. As if that made it any less of a killer mark. His father was going to burn down the single wide. This was *so* not all right.

Lifting the front pages with a trembling hand, Salva flipped through the essay. Maybe he'd deleted a paragraph without realizing it. Or maybe he'd switched the latter half with Pepe's chem lab report. But no—nothing was missing.

"Mundane" was the only comment the Mercenary had bothered to insert.

He couldn't remember the last time he'd gotten a D. Or even a C. Well, there had been that health project last year in which the class had been told to film public-service announcements; but that had been a group assignment, and he couldn't be responsible for pulling everyone up to his level. He hadn't even been allowed to choose his group members. But that was one of those hokey projects worth about 2 percent of his grade.

This was different. And the D was all his.

He left his front page folded over so no one could see the mark and let his focus drift over to Luka. Who was not dying. A thick green B- was displayed for all to see square in the center of his desk.

"You got a B?" Salva whispered.

Luka raised an eyebrow. "Is that supposed to make me feel bad?"

"No, man, I barely even *passed.*"

"Seriously?"

Salva didn't have to respond to that because the Mercenary had finished dispensing her hemlock and was making her way back to the front of the room.

"Overall," she said, her flinty eyes seeming to drill right into him, "I thought you had a lot more potential."

Salva's gaze sought refuge in the ceiling. There was something much safer in looking at the overhead panels with their hundred holes per square than in watching a teacher on a power trip.

"Some of you," she went on, "actually wrote nice little elementary-school essays with five sentences per paragraph, five paragraphs per essay, and a thesis that started with "My essay is about . . ." Real anger grated in her voice.

He pressed his spine against the upper edge of his chair. At least someone had done worse than him.

"Most of you just wrote tripe."

His gaze fell.

Tripe? Luka mouthed.

BS, Salva interpreted. And, well, yeah, what essay wasn't BS? Did teachers really think students today didn't have better things to do than analyze classics that had been read and reread a billion times? If there was anything worthwhile to say about *Paradise Lost,* it had been said three hundred years ago, and Salva really didn't care to improve on it.

"The *point* of an essay"—the Mercenary's face had turned the shade of an overripe apricot—"is to analyze the literary work in a *meaningful* way, and to apply to it one's own unique perspective. Or vice versa."

She was messing with language now. Letting it mean what she wanted it to mean and pretending that was an excuse for communication. Salva prepared to tune her out.

Except he really couldn't afford to get a D in this class.

Which meant he was going to have to listen to this woman. So he could learn how to write for her. Maybe he wasn't God's gift to writing genius, but he knew where to put quotes and commas. For most teachers, that would get you an A right there. And he always made sure he had three pages, a thesis, and a clear beginning, middle, and end. What more did she want?

It was an essay, *por amor de Dios.* There was no purpose to an essay. It was just one of those things teachers invented so they could torture you with them. And he was as good at following the rules as the next guy, so maybe not an A. But a *D?*

The Mercenary parked herself in front of the walking disaster area. Beth Courant was just as much of a mess sitting as she was walking. Her backpack lay sideways, jammed halfway under her desk and open, spilling not one, but three loose-leaf notebooks, about twenty pencils, a calculator, and spiraled bits of paper. Not to mention a very torn-up copy of a romance novel titled *A Long and Fatal Love Chase* that had made its way out into the sacred teaching zone in front of the Mercenary's foot.

Salva tensed for the explosion.

"Ms. Courant, here," the Mercenary said, "seems to be the only one of you with the creative guts to go out on a limb and break it off." She picked up the half-stained paper from Beth's desk and raised it into the air like the Union flag in *The Red Badge of Courage*. At the top of the paper, there was a huge green A. "Here she argues that by describing the worlds of heaven and hell, purgatory and earth in vivid detail, Milton defies the schism between science and religion and bridges the space-time continuum."

My God. Salva cringed. If he was going to have to come up with a thesis like that, he might as well drop out now and start paying union dues at the onion plant.

"Fortunately for the rest of you, I allow students to revise their first piece of work."

Why? So you can drip poison all over it again?

He returned his gaze to the ceiling and began to invent geometric proofs with the holes in the panels. The rest of the class period dragged by like an overblown big-budget movie with a series of false endings. When the bell finally rang, Salva didn't trust his own senses.

"Don't worry." Luka elbowed him. "This, too, shall pass. Ya know, I got a B."

"How?" Salva grimaced. If the running back claimed, like the Mercenary's star pupil, to have interpreted a bridge through the space-time continuum, then maybe this was all a nightmare and morning would come to the rescue.

Luka chuckled. "How do you think?" He nodded toward Nalani.

Ah. The correct study partner. Salva surveyed the tall girl with the dark Italian-Hawaiian features. She was decent enough looking, he supposed, if you ignored the straitjacket posture, her failure to follow through with things, and her color-coded notes.

"Don't get any ideas," Luka added. "She's *my* study partner. You get your own."

Nalani filed away her notebook and reached down to retrieve the romance novel for her best friend, the walking disaster area, who gave a brilliant smile and started yammering away without seeming to notice she had just set her calculator on the desk beside her. Heads together, both girls left the room, leaving the calculator behind.

The Mercenary's stupid metaphor rang in Salva's head: *The only one with the creative guts to go out on the limb and break it off.*

Luka trailed after the girls.

Salva flipped his essay back to the front page and gave a long hard look at that D. Which shifted into visions of a burning single wide, a lifetime at the processing plant, and his father yanking his son off the football team.

D for *desperate.* He scooped up his backpack, wove his way around two desks, and retrieved the abandoned calculator.

I am an utter *failure.* Beth stared down at the poster beneath her. The words *Sell, sell, sell!* sprawled across the white paper as though painted by a three-year-old. How in a nine-hour period could she travel from triumph to devastation? This morning, when her essay had been quoted, she had felt like nothing in the world could hold her down, and now . . . she had been defeated by a few simple fund-raising posters.

Her knees ached. School had been over for an hour and a half, and she had been here, alone, crouched down on the hard surface of the multipurpose room stage for the whole time. All to achieve nothing better than this.

Perhaps I'm exaggerating.

Though not much. She scanned her previous endeavors, then leaned back.

And dripped golden paint halfway across the current poster.

At that moment *he* appeared, in the doorway.

Or perhaps he had been standing there watching her, but that was ridiculous. The most popular guy in school had no reason to watch her. Though he was crossing the room now, quick rapid steps over the tiled floor to the base of the stage. He held out his hand and tried to give her her calculator.

She stared at him. For three reasons. One, her fingers were covered with paint. Two, she couldn't remember the last time he'd come up to her outside of class. *On purpose.* And three, he was soaking wet.

Actually, his hair was soaking. And the rest of him was astoundingly clean for someone who had just gotten out of sports practice. Most guys smelled like sweat and grass-stained football pads when they dragged themselves home at the end of the day. He had showered, obviously. And used cologne.

"You left that behind in English this morning," he said.

Yes, well, she had noticed the calculator was missing during trig. Though in truth, this was the third time in the first two and a half weeks of school, so the loss hadn't exactly ruined her day. "Thank you." She motioned for him to set the calculator down.

Salva gave her a doubtful look, as if to say leaving her stuff lying around was how she lost it. What did he expect? Her to drop everything and run back to her locker on his schedule just because he had chosen to bring her the item now? If he had wanted to be helpful, he could have brought it to her *before* trig.

Then again, maybe he was eyeing her because she was still dripping golden paint on the ASB fund-raising poster. *Argh!*

His gaze fell to the disastrous sign, and she saw the jolt

suddenly run through his body. His index finger traced the base of the crookedly painted words, as though trying to straighten them out. "Isn't this Nalani's job?" he asked.

Beth ventured to explain. "She has yearbook, so I'm helping out." *A lot of help I'm being.*

He reached forward and literally guided her brush to its Styrofoam paint cup. "You're not in yearbook?"

She shuddered at the thought of what the scrapbook-oriented members of the yearbook club would have said in response to that.

"I'm in drama," she replied, "which doesn't start till next week. But Ms. Kinsey said I could use the stage tonight while I was waiting for Ni."

He scrambled up onto the stage, then cringed as he eyed her work. "Can't you be in both drama and yearbook?" he asked.

"I'm pretty busy"—Beth terminated that line of the conversation. "Especially this fall, with college and scholarship applications."

"Mmm-hmm." He moved back and forth at the base of her current poster, then crouched down, lifted a thin paintbrush, and dipped it into a cup with blue paint. "So you know where you're applying yet?"

"Stanford."

He dropped the brush. *Well!* Gods weren't perfect either.

"That's ambitious." Salva lifted the brush with care, leaving an almost invisible mark.

How was that possible?

He began to outline the letters. *Fixing* them. "You seem pretty certain about where you want to go," he said.

"Oh, I'm trying a bunch of places, but Stanford has the best English program on the West Coast."

"According to someone."

"According to me." She smiled. "And I'm the only one who matters."

He was silent for a moment, etching a nearly perfect curve around the *S* in the first *Sell*. She felt like she was in one of those cheesy sci-fi shows where all the characters wake up in a different dimension. What was he doing here? Helping her with posters after an hour and a half of football practice. He must be wiped. And it wasn't like any of *his* friends were in yearbook.

"Listen," he said.

A queasy warning turned in the pit of her stomach. He wanted something from her. People didn't get to the top of the popularity echelon without knowing how to use others to their advantage.

"I know you're really good at English," he said.

Yes, that was how things always started. *Begin with the compliment, and then move on to hitting me up.* That was how Beth had wound up painting posters on the stage, though Nalani was a friend. With friends this kind of thing was mutual.

But Salva Resendez? He didn't know Beth existed. Not in

the social sphere at least. They had taken a bunch of classes together, though not that many this year since he was into the kill-yourself science and math courses, and she was more into the take-enough-science-and-math-this-year-so-you-don't-have-to-take-them-next-year mind-set.

But they were both in cit/gov, career prep, and—

"Markham says I have no choice but to take AP English."

Her paintbrush left a nasty golden streak in the middle of an attempt to repair the earlier damage. Salva had never struck her as the kind of person who quit. "You tried to drop it?" she asked.

"I didn't sign up for it in the first place," he said. "I figured since we took senior English last year, I was done." He groaned. "But Markham says I have to take four years of high school English *in high school* to graduate. So I'm stuck."

Yeah, he pretty much was, she realized. There had been a couple other English electives offered at Liberty in the past, but they had all either been dumped or switched to after-school programs in order to pump up the number of remedial and AP courses.

"Sorry," she said, then knew at once that had been the wrong thing to say, because he was no longer painting a perfect blue outline, but was looking her square in the eye. At least he had the guts to look at her.

"I got a D on my essay today."

She did not say *sorry* again, though she did think it, this time with more sincerity because she knew Salva never turned in D work. D implied Did Not Try, though the Mercenary was known to ignore that rule.

"I was hoping you might help me," he continued. "I really . . ." The perfect veneer was gone, and for a moment he looked like the scared little kid she remembered from his first week of English immersion in the third grade—the boy who had run crying to the teacher because he'd thought the automatic toilets in the modern bathroom were going to swallow him. "I can't afford not to pass this class."

"You'll pass," she said, feeling a sudden urge to comfort him, which was so *not safe* while she was sitting across from those deep brown eyes. Which belonged to the ASB president, she reminded herself. There was no reason to feel sorry for him. With all the AP courses he took, his GPA would probably be higher than hers even if he did earn a D in English. Which was saying something, since she hadn't earned less than an A- in her entire high-school career. "The Mercenary is just trying to scare people so she can get better work throughout the course."

He did not look comforted. He looked like that pitiful third grader, save for the long, well-defined limbs of a high-school senior. "Please," he said.

Please? How could good manners be so devastating? But they were. Really. How many guys at Liberty High ever said, "Please"? Or brought a girl her calculator? Or helped with her work?

He just wants something. That doesn't count.

Or picked her papers up after she spilled them all over the hallway the first day of school?

This was not good. This was so not good. She knew she had been thinking about that incident too much, and here it had come back to bite her.

No way am I going to spend this whole year crushing on the most popular guy in school. I have walked that line before, and it is not healthy. Face it. She had cried her eyes out over him back in middle school. And he had never had a clue.

She had no desire to return to that era.

Not with one year left before he was out of her life. And she could move on from those dark brown eyes and that gorgeous damp hair.

"I don't think tutoring someone after school is going to provide me with more time for applications," she said.

He repeated: "Please."

She bit her lip and painted furiously. *This is not a good idea. This is not a good idea. This is not a good idea.* The long-term quality of her heart was worth more than the short-term compulsion to do what was right. And make him happy.

"Just . . ." he continued, "would you look at my essay from today and maybe tell me what I could have done better? The Mercenary said we could fix our papers, but she didn't write any comments about what to change." Beth could hear the panic rising in his voice. "And I don't know how I'm going to make it better if I don't know what is wrong."

It wasn't fair. That vulnerability. Combined with the desperation in his voice. And the assertion that *he* needed *her*.

"All right." Beth winced as tiny golden spots from her paintbrush sprinkled his nose and chin. Then she sighed at the inanity of her ever having had a crush on someone who was able to function without embarrassing himself on a regular basis. "I'll read it, this *one* essay. That's it."

"Thank you." He smiled and wiped the paint spatters off with his thumb and forefinger, until once again he appeared . . .

Perfect.

Beth faced the initial consequences of her weakness the next morning when he brought her the essay. At her locker. In full view of the entire senior hall. She could feel the incredulous glances and disapproving stares from snob corner. The likes of Linette Kasing and Char Mendoza.

Salva didn't seem to notice, just held out his crisp paper. *He could have given it to me last night,* Beth thought, though she suspected he had been afraid she would lose the essay overnight. Which, frankly, never would have happened. She still had the Valentine's Day card he had given her in the third grade.

But she could not blame him for his fear. She *could* blame him for the fact that Char was pretending to inspect her fingernails by flicking her middle finger in Beth's direction.

Ignore her.

Beth focused on Salva. Who smelled like mint hair gel. He was reeling off more politeness, this time thanking her for being willing to read his paper.

Which she took, then buried her head in her locker, giving him the chance to make a getaway.

Except that he didn't. Instead, he leaned his back on the neighboring locker, dropped his head in a slight clang against the dented metal, and looked at her. Waiting.

As if she was going to read his paper right that second.

"Um . . ." she said. "I'll try to return it by the end of the day."

He glanced at his watch, a neat black band that made him appear, she thought, a little too prepared for the adult world. "We've got ten minutes."

Surely he could not be that terrified of her losing the essay? After all, he must have saved the text on the computer. And probably backed up the file twenty times. "Look," she said, trying not to sound too patronizing, "it might take only ten minutes to read, but then I have to come up with what to say. So unless you want garbage for feedback"—*or to have me rip out your guts when I tell you what's wrong*—"then I'll need more time."

"Well." He rubbed the perfect brown skin on the back of his neck. "After school I've got practice. Are you still going to be here when it's over?"

She certainly hoped not. Nalani might yet have to approve the posters, but Beth was of the opinion they were done. And technically, she had the ASB president's word on that, since he had pronounced them finished when he had left the night before.

"We could talk at lunch." She threw out the idea, knowing

no way was he going to forgo his social ritual at the premier table in order to sit with her.

"Maybe second half?" His eyes lit up. "We could meet in the hall over by the pop machine."

In the out-of-the-way alcove not too far from the cafeteria. "Sure," she said, uncertain if he knew he had just dissed her by failing to invite her to meet up at his table. One of the annoying things about Salva was the way he could give her all the attention in the world, for a moment, then totally exclude her from his life.

But he *was* standing here by her locker.

"Okay." He grinned, running his hand through that dark, gelled hair. "I'll see you at twelve fifteen."

He left. Cutting a long diagonal across the crowd to arm-wrestle Pepe Real.

One of the most annoying guys on the face of the planet.

Pepe slapped him a high five, smacked a huge wad of gum, and made a rude sexual gesture at a girl in a miniskirt.

There alone, Beth thought, was reason to be glad she wasn't cool enough to spend time with Salva Resendez. Her fingers tightened on the essay, and she congratulated herself on not caving to his request to help throughout the entire class. She would just read this one paper and get it over with. Her eyes traced their way over the title. Boring. Did he not understand the purpose of a title?

She flipped the pages, read the teacher's comment, and groaned.

Salva punched the buttons on the pop machine in the rhythm of the fight song. The machine was empty, some law having been passed that teenagers were too stupid to know how much sugar they were putting in their mouths. His fingers slowed, and he let his eyes peruse the valedictorian names on the Academic Wall of Fame. Not a very big wall. Or very large plaques, at least not compared to those on Sports Trophy Row.

Beth was five minutes late, but that wasn't a surprise, considering who he was dealing with. It would be a miracle if she arrived at all. He had known he should have made her read the essay right there at her locker this morning.

She came whipping around the corner. *Whoa!* He hadn't seen her move that fast since she'd given up track.

"In *Paradise Lost*"—she quoted his thesis—"Milton solidified himself as one of the greatest writers of all time through his brilliant portrayal of man's fall from grace." She slapped something that vaguely resembled Salva's old paper into his hand. "You practically plagiarized the Mercenary."

"Yeah, so?" He tried to smooth out the wrinkles. That was the way the game was played. You found out what the teacher thought, and you went along.

"Give me a break." She shifted one of the plaques, setting it off its axis. "Can you honestly say you think Milton is one of the greatest authors you've ever read?"

Claro que no. But that didn't matter. He eyed the bright patch of wall revealed when the plaque had shifted. "The Mercenary thinks he is."

"That's not the point."

Sure it is.

Beth gave a huge sigh. "Look, do you read anything outside of school?"

Did she think he was an idiot? His name was going to be on this half-ass wall if he could survive AP English. "Of course."

"Who are your favorite authors?"

He shrugged, propping his foot on the bench beneath the plaques, then shifted his weight forward and back. He didn't have favorite authors.

"What are you reading right now?" she harped.

A bio on the president's life and a history of Chiapas. "I read nonfiction."

She reared back as if offended.

Well, it's better than romance novels. Though today he had noticed a Stephen King book by her feet.

"Just tell me what you really think of Milton," she said, her arms crossed over her chest. She had his back up now. What had been all that yakking about taking the time to provide him with quality feedback?

"Honestly?" he asked.

Her chin gave a sharp nod.

"I think he's an anti-Catholic, bigoted ass," Salva replied. *Not to mention sexist.* He figured there were plenty of things wrong with Catholicism, but he didn't need to hear about them from a guy who had never been forced to sit through mass on a frigging Wednesday night. And who couldn't even find a way to couch his raging prejudices in an interesting story. Any book that could put Salva to sleep before nine P.M. twice in one week was just not going into his top ten.

"Then *say* that." Beth snapped her fingers and pointed at his chest.

He should have known that someone who read about fatal love chases could not be trusted to give good advice.

"Look," she continued, "the Mercenary doesn't want to hear what she already knows. If you think Milton is a prejudiced ass, then say so—well, don't swear, but say what you think and then back up your argument. Put in the quotes. Analyze the hell out of it. And prove your point. The teacher might disagree with you in theory, but at least she won't be bored. *That*"—Beth waved a hand at his essay—"is a waste of anyone's time."

Salva stared at her blankly.

"Now an essay about Milton's prejudices," she said. "That would be worth reading."

"You're serious?"

"Deadly."

He could deal with that. "All right, I'll bring it to you on Monday."

"What?"

He pushed off the bench. "I'm taking you seriously. I'm trying to 'go out on the limb and break it off,' but I don't have the creative guts to go it alone. And you just said the essay would be worth reading."

She was shaking her head, then bit her bottom lip.

"Please," he added.

He had her. He knew it. There was no way she could just allow him to write trash for the rest of the year.

The bit lip transformed into a slow nod.

Now the only question was whether her advice was worth anything. Or whether following it would get him lynched.

Beth berated herself all the way home, the trek longer than normal due to a detour to the grocery store. A milk jug weighed down her left hand, and plastic bags bit into her wrists—a fitting punishment for her failure of will. Why couldn't she say no to him? *Why?* It wasn't the manners, not really. They were just an excuse. And it wasn't that he'd die without her help. He'd aced every English class he'd had before this one. He would be fine. Not what he was capable of, but fine. Though it burned her to see him hover just below spectacular.

She kicked a piece of asphalt across the street. Toward the trailer.

The screen door was open. Beth froze, staring at it, trying to remember if she'd turned the lock that morning. *There's nothing inside. At least nothing worth a payoff for a thief or a meth addict.*

Then she noticed the beaten-up, orange Oldsmobile parked almost on the curb. Her mother was home. For the first time before eleven P.M. all week.

Beth crossed the street and stepped through the doorway.

"Where have you been?" Ms. Courant looked up from the open fridge. Her drab brown hair was pulled back in a flat tail, and she'd exchanged her uniform for a shirt with a rip in the hem. Crow's-feet marred her eyes, the lines on her face deep for a woman only in her mid-thirties. "And what are you carrying?"

Beth's heart sank as she realized her mother had also gone shopping. There were two milk jugs and four grocery bags already on the counter. Beth had known it was a risk to go herself. But she'd had little choice. With the dearth of food in the trailer, it had been either that or invite herself over to Nalani's for dinner a second night in a row.

Her mother wrestled with one of the fridge drawers, then slammed it shut. "Just what are we supposed to do with three gallons of milk?"

Which meant Beth wasn't getting reimbursed.

"I . . . I didn't know if you—"

"If I noticed there wasn't milk for cereal this morning? You might have picked some up yesterday. If you were concerned."

The whistle on the kettle began to scream.

"I used my summer's work money," Beth said.

"Good." Her mother left the fridge and hustled across the linoleum to lift the kettle. "It's about time you pitched in." She snagged the plastic coffee funnel and began rummaging in a drawer.

Beth moved up to the cupboards, dug into one of her sacks, pulled out a box of coffee filters, and slid it across the counter, then began putting away groceries from both sets of bags. She shelved three jars of the same marinara sauce, four sacks of the same pasta, and two bags of the same generic cereal. At least she hadn't wasted what she'd spent on fruit. Her mother never splurged on fresh produce.

The sound of dripping from the coffee filter derailed Beth's focus. "Look, honey"—Ms. Courant used the term *honey* only as a diminutive—"don't you think you could at least pick up around here? I spend all day cleaning at that high-priced hotel. I really don't have time to clean for you, too." She chucked the coffee funnel into the sink: paper, grounds, and all.

Don't argue, Beth told herself. *She'll just use it against you.* At least her mother hadn't been drinking—not since the funeral. But she was never home. And when she was, she was always tired. Or stressed because there wasn't enough money.

Beth shoved a couple sacks of frozen vegetables into the freezer, then flicked on the radio.

Fuzz blared.

"It's broken," her mother said.

It had worked yesterday. Beth reached for the antennae.

"Not now." Her mother toted the coffee cup out of the kitchen zone and slumped down on the sagging couch. She kicked off her shoes without untying them. "I have homework," she said, making no move to retrieve any supplies. "Don't *you* have any?"

"I have an application." *But I thought you wanted me to clean.*

"An application for what?"

"Regional college." Beth opened the cupboard door and retrieved the garbage can. The smell was noxious.

Her mother's hand tightened on the back of her own neck. "Well, that would be a waste of your grandfather's savings."

Dammit. Beth took out the garbage.

It wasn't her fault: the college trust—the fund no one could get their hands on except to pay for Beth's education.

Her grandfather had had money. At one time.

He'd owned a big cattle ranch outside of town and run most of it into the ground, but he'd set aside enough in a trust for Beth to use *if* she went to college. It was her mother's money, really—had belonged to her mother for a whole first semester at Notre Dame. Until she had come home pregnant.

And Beth's grandfather had sealed off every cent.

She isn't angry at you, Grandma would have said. *She's angry at him.*

Beth lifted the lid on the outside trash container, dumped in the odorous garbage, and shut the top. Then forced herself to breathe.

I didn't ask for the money. And I'm not going to feel sorry about it. She hauled the emptied can back through the screen door. Might as well get this discussion out of the way now. She spoke:

"Regional is my safety school. I'm going to Stanford."

"Oh." Her mother's laugh was bitter. "Of course."

Stanford was Beth's grandfather's alma mater. He'd wanted his daughter to go there, but she hadn't wanted any part of it. Beth didn't know why. She figured it had something to do with wishing you would not become your parents.

Or parent, in her own case.

But her mother's battles weren't Beth's.

Family connections meant something at expensive schools. And it didn't matter if the connection was someone your mother hated. Beth shoved the trash container into its cupboard, then plucked the plastic filter from the sink, dumped out the paper and coffee grounds, and turned on the faucet, letting the sound drown out the silence behind her.

Maybe it wasn't fair: attending a school that would cost twenty times what it would cost to put both her mother and her through community college. But Beth hadn't made the rules. And she hadn't broken them. She hadn't been the one to throw away her chance at an education in exchange for an ill-fated relationship with some guy who had never forfeited anything. And she wasn't going to allow her mother's bitterness to ruin her own dreams.

After all, Beth's mother would eventually be glad when her daughter left the trailer. At least then there'd be a drop in the grocery bill. And one less person to remind Ms. Courant of the mistake that had wrecked her entire existence.

6

MY LIFE HAD STOOD—A
LOADED GUN

Death, death, death.

The poems were all about death. Salva flipped through the ten-ton *Norton Anthology*, the practiced walls of his mind faltering in their attempt to shut out the humid space, cramped quarters, and banging clatter of the Laundromat. A nearby infant girl in her mother's arms started to scream. Salva frowned. He'd spent enough Tuesday nights here, completing the family chore, that he could usually block out everything.

"Dickinson or Frost," his study partner had suggested yesterday at their second session. "Keep your hands off Whitman. He's mine."

As if I'd argue over the rights to some dead poet. Salva had earned a B on his Milton revision. Enough to convince him the walking disaster area's advice was worth heeding as he faced the Mercenary's current mode of torture—an analysis of any poem by any poet from any era. He *hated* assignments without clear parameters. Which was why he'd asked Beth for advice.

And he'd *intended* to follow it.

Before he began to read. And flip. And read.

His stomach rumbled, and he pressed his left hand to the football-practice-induced ache at the back of his neck.

This wasn't working. This wasn't going to work.

Even the poems with the happy titles. "After Apple-Picking" —what right did that have to be about death?

He didn't like Frost.

"Salva!" Talia's voice rang out. His name was followed by the double banging of his younger sisters coming through the Laundromat door.

He shot a glance at his watch: 6:30 P.M. They weren't supposed to be here. Char was supposed to keep them until eight o'clock on Monday and Tuesday nights. Salva had sibling duty on Wednesdays and Thursdays. That was the deal *los padres* had made after getting their new shift schedules.

Casandra reached him first. A compact, passionate bundle of nine-year-old drama. "Today was the most awful day!" she declared, plowing into his stomach and sweeping her arms around his neck.

He dropped the anthology on the bench and endeavored to follow her words as she outlined the nuances of fourth-grade social structure—something about a friendship bracelet she had spent hours slaving away over for the new girl in class.

"And then"—Talia arrived to take over the account—"I found it in the trash!" She stood, shoulders back, arms crossed over her chest. A slightly taller, more intense version of her ten-month-older sister. He had no doubt, based on their tone, that throwing away a friendship bracelet was the ultimate betrayal in nine-year-old-girl speak.

Salva let them talk for the duration of a laundry cycle. He did his best to empathize over the bracelet thing, asked about their Girl Scout meeting, and checked over Talia's homework.

Which reminded him he had a paper to write. And if he didn't start, he was going to wind up screwed. He had only an hour in the computer lab this week for typing up the revision, and he couldn't go in early for extra access since he had to drop the girls off at their bus. Unless he called Char and asked her to take them. Which—no kidding—she owed him after shorting his time tonight.

But he couldn't help thinking she had ditched the girls early on purpose so that he would have to call. And he wasn't going there. When Char latched onto a tactic that helped her achieve what she wanted, she didn't know when to quit.

He interrupted the third reprise of the Tale of the Friendship Bracelet to ask his sisters if they'd had dinner.

Both nodded. *At least Char didn't sketch on that.*

He pointed them toward an empty spot on the half-open bench across from him. "Okay, then go read," he said, "or draw or make another set of bracelets. I have to study. If you're good, I'll make tacos for breakfast." Their eyebrows rose, no doubt because Salva wasn't so hot at cooking. He could fry up bacon, potatoes, chilies, and onions, though, and stick them in a tortilla.

"Or we could study this together." He hefted the *Norton Anthology*.

Both girls eyed the massive book with identical horror, then retreated.

Salva opened up the anthology.

Ten seconds later tween pop music came from the Laundromat radio.

His head flew up to see Casandra dancing, dangerously close to a vibrating dryer.

"Turn it off!" he yelled.

The mothers in the room began to whisper, and the peeling wall poster of the Virgen de Guadalupe seemed to frown at him.

But the sound lessened. Marginally. He rubbed his neck again. He shouldn't have yelled. Lucia would hear about it, then scold him when she came home from community college. And he'd take it from his older sister because he deserved it.

But at least Casandra was sitting now.

He opened the book back to Emily Dickinson. She didn't mess around like Frost—didn't play with titles and pretend her poems were about something happy when they weren't. Just started in with her own versions of brutality.

My Life had stood—a Loaded Gun . . .

Because I could not stop for Death . . .

I felt a funeral in my brain . . .

I heard a fly buzz when I died . . .

The words of the fourth poem drilled through the hard knot

in Salva's stomach. He could hear that fly of death. He *had* heard it. It was the reason he was here. The reason his sisters had to be traded back and forth between houses in the evening. The reason *Papá* had to work such long hours.

That was a hell of a poem.

No way could Salva write about it.

He swallowed the F—digested the green felt-tip poison as soon as the graded paper landed on his desk. *Poems are about emotion,* the walking disaster area had told him. *Just write about the meaning and what it makes you feel.*

He had ignored her, point-blank.

A second paper hit his desk. For a moment he thought maybe the Mercenary was assigning him extra work because he had failed so miserably.

But she passed out the same photocopy to the person in front of him and the person in front of that. They couldn't all be as inept as he was.

"I thought," the Mercenary said, her heels clicking as she continued down the rows, "that since most of you work harder to impress one another than your teachers, you might all benefit from seeing what one of your peers can accomplish. You may read it on your own. I assume all of you are capable of that, at least."

Salva looked down at the photocopy. He couldn't focus. He'd never in his life gotten an F. Maybe he should try retaking freshman lit. Markham couldn't force him to stay here, could he?

Of course he can. One call to Papá and I'm a scorched enchilada stuck to the pan.

No friends. No football. Nothing except AP English.

The Mercenary was talking again, blathering about dark romantics versus bright romantics. Salva blocked her out.

And the printed words on the photocopy finally slid into focus. "Out of the Cradle Endlessly Rocking: A Song of Reincarnation."

The paper was about death.

Not the death Dickinson wrote about but still real—the death of something so beautiful that the narrator could no longer stay the same person after witnessing the loss.

And the writer got it.

Not the poet—though Whitman probably did—but the author of the essay, who argued that the narrator had to change. Because that was how death worked. You couldn't just go on being who you were before, after losing something that important.

"At least I can't." The paper ended.

Salva read through the conclusion twice.

She'd lost someone. Seen them die right before her eyes. Not the final moment, maybe, but all the moments leading up to it. And all the days after when that someone wasn't there.

And she'd done exactly what she had told Salva to do— written about how it made her feel. He pulled his gaze away from the final line and found himself staring at Beth.

Who had she lost?

—

"An F?!" Beth gasped. *How could* you *have gotten an F?* The roll of masking tape dropped from her hands, and she checked her balance in her crouched position on the stage. Okay, she hadn't had time to read his paper because of the tight deadline, but she'd given Salva all the advice that was necessary. "What did you write about?"

"'Jabberwocky.'"

"What?!"

"The poem 'Jabberwocky,' from *Alice in Wonderland*—well, *Through the Looking-Glass* actually. Listen, it's not your fault."

It darn well wasn't. She scooped up the tape and unrolled it in a sharp slash, forming the final X for drama club rehearsals, then began looking for her stuff. She hadn't risked her mental health by agreeing to meet him here every Monday so that he could ignore her advice and write a three-page paper about a monster from a poem about nonsense.

"It was a stupid idea," he said.

She was the one who had been stupid. Why had he bothered to ask for her help? Was this some dare like in the movies where the guy hung out with the loser girl only because his buddies said they'd pay up? Or because someone told him she was easy?

Right, Beth. Like he'd ever think of you in that context.

Notebook, pencils, folders—she gathered them from the

corners of the stage, stuffing the items into her backpack without regard for where they went.

"Look," he said, "I got the grade I deserve, I know."

Her copy of Elizabeth Gaskell's *North and South*.

"I really do need your help."

Sure he did. Maybe this situation was good. Maybe this would finally get through to her idiotic heart.

Beth shoved the book into her backpack, zipped the pocket as far as it would close, and headed for the multipurpose room exit.

"Hey, wait!" At last he seemed to catch on to the fact that she was leaving. "Please."

"If you *think*—" She stopped at the door, reining herself in. There was no point in yelling. Really. He had no inkling of what she had risked by being here. She exhaled, then continued, "I'm sure you can find someone else to help you with your homework."

Whom had she been kidding? Of course he could.

Stupid. Stupid. Stupid.

Beth pushed the handle on the door.

And something hit the floor behind her.

That dumb calculator! He beat her to it. "Listen," he said, palming the device. "I just wanted to say, well . . ."

She didn't want to listen—didn't need to listen. Let him flunk the class!

"That took guts," he said.

Walking away from you?

"The paper," he clarified. "The one the Mercenary shared with us today. You wrote it, didn't you?"

All the certainty in Beth's flight deflated. How had he known the paper was hers? The teacher had folded over the name in the top corner before running copies.

But, of course, Beth had told *him* she was writing about Whitman.

"Who was it?" he asked softly. "The person who died?"

And Beth breathed. "My grandma."

He tilted his head. "The one who lived with you?"

That was a surprise. Beth hadn't expected him to remember her grandmother. "Yes."

"When did she die?" he asked.

Beth would have backed away, except the door was right behind her, and . . . walking out on someone who was asking about Grandma wasn't okay. "This summer."

He reached out slowly. Then instead of handing over Beth's calculator, he lifted the strap of her backpack off her shoulder and pulled the pack from her arm. "She used to come to the school sometimes, right?" he asked.

"Yes." Beth blinked. Grandma had always been the one to find time to attend plays and conferences.

He sat down, crossed his legs on the floor, and slid the calculator into the back pocket, then tried, futilely, to close the zipper. All the zippers were bad. "What was she like?"

"She was awesome."

He unzipped the main section of the backpack and started ripping out the cheap vinyl seam binding that always caught on the metal teeth before the zipper would close. "What was awesome about her?"

And Beth found herself spilling. About the silliest things: the snappy comments her grandmother had used to wake Beth when she forgot to set the alarm, the mystery dessert Grandma had packed when they had picnicked down by the river, the way she used to stun the braggarts at the tavern by correcting them when they misquoted rodeo stats.

Salva listened. Politely. Though Beth couldn't quite read the expression on his face. It was the strangest thing, but he actually seemed to want to hear.

No one else did. Her mother always took offense. Like Beth's missing her grandmother was some kind of personal attack. And Ni—Beth could tell when her friend was uncomfortable. Death wasn't something a whole lot of people wanted to talk about.

Not that Salva was talking, just asking a few questions as, one by one, he opened all the pockets on the backpack and fixed the zippers. He didn't return the pack until Beth stopped spilling memories.

Then he glanced at his wristwatch, an action that made her look at the clock: 6:35 P.M. She'd talked all the way through a normal tutoring session! "So," he said, his eyes back on her face, "next Monday? Same time? Same place?"

Beth hesitated, then nodded slowly. She wanted to forgive him. Because he had listened. Today. But he had still ignored her advice about the poetry analysis. "Why do you want my help if you're going to disregard it?" she asked.

His gaze remained unreadable. "That essay about your grandmother—that took guts to write. I couldn't."

He couldn't what?

"What did she die of?" he asked.

"Cancer."

The wince on his face was so sharp Beth finally read the emotion. *Pain.*

Oh God, she was an idiot.

She'd totally forgotten about his mother.

HOMECOMING

God had probably, Beth told herself, given her a brain so she could avoid spending the last Friday night in October freezing her ass off on the bleachers. Her eyes hinged on the number 8, the blue print on the gold jersey still visible under the lights of the football field. Barely. The fog had begun to sink early in the homecoming game. Her legs and arms were numb beneath her grandmother's chiffon vintage dress, and huddling closer to Nalani did nothing to decrease the chill.

Ni was watching number 12, Luka, who had finally gotten up the guts to ask her out a week ago, which meant *she* had a date to the dance after the game and, therefore, was compelled to watch him play.

So why am I here?

Nalani had pleaded with her best friend to come, and, despite Beth's apathy toward football, a few hours of sipping hot chocolate above the stands in Ni's parents' Blazer had seemed like a reasonable request. But it had been too foggy to see from the bluff, and Ni, afraid she might miss Luka's touchdowns, had insisted both she and her friend move down to the stands, where they could watch their breath fog.

Which really was going too far.

No rule in the bond of friendship had demanded Beth exit that warm Blazer to freeze.

Though she had. To be honest, the choice had nothing to do with Nalani. And everything to do with Beth's own sick compulsion to watch that distant number 8 hurl a ball.

Her teeth chattered. "What time . . . is the dance?" she asked.

"Oh, about ten o'clock," Ni replied, hugging herself despite a thick burgundy sweater. "Whenever the game is over and the guys are ready. You're coming, aren't you?" She glanced at her friend. "You're already dressed."

Beth shook her head. She didn't know why she had put on the thin gown. Except that everyone thought of the game as a celebration. It had seemed like a good excuse to wear her grandmother's dress—at least that had been Beth's line of thinking this afternoon when she had gone home to a pile of dirty laundry. And a clothes dryer that required three separate starts to complete a load. "I don't like school dances," she said. *If you don't have a date, you just watch everyone else dance. And pray you get asked once or twice.*

Beth was incapable of asking a guy to dance.

Besides, I'm busy mooning over the one I most definitely cannot have.

She should have turned Salva down flat that first day. Then

she wouldn't have caved later. And if she hadn't spent every Monday study session with him for the past month and half, she wouldn't be freezing now.

Three years she'd been trying to convince herself that her middle-school crush hadn't been real. That he was just a superficial image on whom she'd pinned all the romantic qualities in her eighth-grade mind.

But he wasn't.

God knew he *was* attractive.

Though she could have gotten past that.

She couldn't get past the fact that he could analyze Tolstoy. At least he could when she challenged him into it.

And he *cared* about people. He'd taken five minutes in the middle of last week's study session to call the food bank and start organizing a Christmas donation effort—even though it was only the end of October.

"Oh, come on, Beth!" Ni touched the filmy fabric on her best friend's short sleeves. "You really should come to the dance. You look beautiful."

No one looked beautiful at this temperature. "You'll be with Luka all night," Beth responded. "You won't even realize I'm not there." The truth. Though she chastised herself, knowing the words had the flavor of jealousy.

Nalani didn't appear to notice, instead latching onto the mention of her new boyfriend. "Did you know he's liked me since last year?"

Beth feigned astonishment, though truthfully, who in the

71

entire school had not noted the running back trailing her best friend?

No verbal response required, Ni launched into a long-winded adoration fest.

And allowed Beth to watch the game. Or rather watch number 8, who motioned for his teammates to huddle, disappeared in their midst, and emerged to take his position. Then the ball launched like a bullet out of his perfect hands.

And into the arms of number 12.

Both Beth and Nalani leaped to their feet, screaming and making enough fog to bury the bleachers.

"Whoooeee!" Pepe yelled, his voice echoing in the steaming locker room. "On to state. On to state." He started the chant over the roar of the final shower.

"On to state. On to state." The deep voices of the team swelled the room. Feet pounded the floor, and several guys jumped off the tops of benches.

Salva pulled on a clean shirt, then picked up his helmet and ran it against the lockers. "Woohoo!" he added to the chant.

"Watch out!" Tosa, half dressed, signaled from across the room, then sprinted over the cement and leaped four feet to chest-butt Pepe.

Shouts erupted and the celebration continued, with Pepe, still in his underwear, as the master of ceremonies.

Salva tied his shoes, slapped on the cologne he usually reserved for mass, and tightened his wristwatch. "Hey!" he shouted, around the antics of his best friend, at Luka. "You going to the after-game party at Linette's?" Rumor had it this party was parent-sponsored, which meant high-quality snacks had been purchased with parental knowledge before her dad and stepmom had left town.

"Nah, I'm going to the dance," said the fully dressed running back, closing his duffel bag.

Pepe laughed. "Wonder who with." He reached out toward the shorter guy's chest and flipped up Luka's tie.

Miss Color-Coded Notes. The running back had been doing his sprints in the air all week. Salva had forgotten. "You could come by after," he said. "It'll probably still be going on."

"I'm guessin' he might have *plans* after," Pepe crowed, beating his bare chest.

Luka ignored the comment, hefted the duffel bag, and vacated the locker room.

Wise. Which showed he really did have brains.

"How 'bout you, Tos?" Pepe elbowed Tosa, who was now tying on his shoe. "You and the hostess have any *plans?*"

"Knock it off, Real," Salva said, rolling his *R* and putting an end to that line of discussion. "Get your ass changed, or we're never gonna get there."

That didn't shut Pepe up, but it did get him to switch topics. And to stick one leg into his jeans. "D'you tell your dad you were going to Linette's?" he asked Salva.

Hell, no. My father thinks gorgeous blondes are the devil incarnate. "I told him I'm spending the night with Tosa."

"Yeah, and what'd you tell yours, Tos?"

"I told my parents I'm going to the dance. What'd you tell your mom?" Tosa flipped the question.

"I told her I was going to the party."

"And she was fine with that?"

"Are you kiddin' me?" Pepe pulled up his jeans and zipped them. By now the rest of the locker room had emptied out. "Tonight, I can do whatever the hell I want. It's my birthday."

Pepe's mom was as white as they came. You'd never have known it to look at Salva's best friend, but you could sure as heck tell by the way he acted. He got away with murder.

"You are so stinkin' spoiled, man," Tosa said.

"Oh, you ain't seen nothin'." Pepe slowly dragged his arms into his cotton shirt. "Wait till you see the present I got from my grandparents."

Tosa met Salva's eyes.

They shared a mutual loathing, and appreciation, for Pepe's grandparents' gifts. As a matter of principle, it was disgusting how much Pepe got for nothing. He'd always had it easy, skipping out of his chores, slacking off in school, then reaping everything from brand-name footballs to professional baseball tickets.

But practically speaking, well, one thing you had to give Pepe credit for: he shared.

"What present?" Salva asked.

"Meet me by the street at the end of the bleachers in ten," his best friend replied. "You'll find out."

"Oh, come on," Tosa said. "We've *been* waiting on your sorry ass."

"Well, I'll make it up to you." Pepe winked.

Again Salva and Tosa exchanged glances. Yeah, they could probably handle this.

The grass along the field's edges was covered in frost, but there were still a few groupies hanging around, waiting to say "Congratulations." Salva appreciated the gesture and tried to be polite, even though he thought there was something a little sad about forty-year-old men who had nothing better to do with their nights than hang out at a high-school football field.

The scary thing was he could totally see Tosa and Pepe doing that in twenty years.

But for me, I am going to find something better to do with my life.

It was one thing to play in the final game before the state championships. That was a rush. Salva was a part of the action, and he wouldn't have given the moment up for anything.

But to spend his future sponging off somebody else's rush? He could do better. He really *had* to do better.

"Hey, Luka's still here." Tosa pointed.

Sure enough, the running back was over at the end of the bleachers, chatting up Nalani. In the same spot selected for the meeting with Pepe.

"Let's interrupt." Tosa yanked Salva by the arm.

Ah, yes, because that is always fun. Of course, with Tosa it usually was.

"Incoming!" The goofy guy proved his rep by bending down and ramming his head toward Luka.

Who reached out with his hands and managed to block, but flew back anyway, propelled by the bigger guy's momentum. The two wrestled for about half a second.

Tosa might not have the mental reflexes to play first string, but he had no trouble overpowering the shorter running back. Holding Luka's head down, he straightened his own six-foot-plus frame and spoke to the restrained-guy's girlfriend. "What'd ya say? Decent entertainment?"

"Congrats, Tosa," said Nalani. "You played great."

"Yeah, I sit the bench really well. It'd float off if I wasn't on it, ya know."

Nalani laughed.

And Tosa, preening at her reaction, must have loosened his grip because Luka ducked and managed to jump away, then swung his right arm around his girlfriend's waist and pulled her in front of him.

She didn't seem to mind being his blocker.

Within seconds, Tosa was showing off for both of them, walking on his hands and spouting his latest comedy act, which Salva had heard about a million times.

A familiar female voice came from behind him. "Y-you played really well, Salva."

He turned, and stared. *Beth.* She stepped forward from the edge of the bleachers. Her teeth were chattering and she was shivering, her hair a strange shade of auburn under the lights, her face drained of color except for her brown eyes. She was wearing a long white gauzelike dress. *My God.* She must be freezing.

He had an instinctive urge to hand over his jacket. Though that would be a total blunder in the social code. You didn't give a girl your jacket unless you were dating. "Um . . . thanks," he said, then feeling like a complete ass, went with the obvious. "You look frozen."

"It w-wasn't this cold at five o'clock," Beth said.

Which probably meant something in her world, but Salva had no idea what.

He shot a glance over at Nalani. It seemed like she'd taken this best friend thing too far, making Beth stand out here freezing while she, herself, was flirting with Luka. Why were they still here? They were all obviously going to the dance.

"I guess the dance'll be heated," Salva said loudly, trying to send the message to the happy couple still laughing at Tosa's comedy act.

"Um . . . sure," Beth replied. There were goose bumps all the way up her arms.

This is stupid, he thought, then reached for the zipper at his throat.

But darkness closed over his eyes, and a curved female form pressed against his back. "Guess who?" Hot air breathed on his cheek. *Char.* She slid her hands down the outline of his face, then linked them low around his neck. And propped her chin on his shoulder. *When was she going to get the message?*

He disconnected the strangling fingers.

She slid forward, her hip glued to his side.

And he pulled away.

Leaving her facing Beth. "What is that you're wearing?" Char mocked the white dress. "A *quinceañera* petticoat from the nineties?" He knew the sarcasm was her response to his rejection. She worked so hard to fit in sometimes she got carried away. But he didn't want her hurting people because of him.

"It was my grandmother's," Beth said, pride full in her voice.

Maybe he ought to intervene.

The other girl sneered. "Well, you should tell your grand-mother to take it with her to the grave."

"Shut up, Char," Salva said. *Too late.*

Beth's eyes had widened, and she had stumbled backward.

Around them everyone had frozen: Luka, Nalani. Even Tosa.

A car horn broke the awkward moment. "Hey, what are you dweebs standin' around out in the cold for?" Pepe yelled.

Char detached herself from the situation and headed toward the voice.

Tosa also shifted in that direction.

Salva's focus remained on Beth, his mind a verbal blank. He couldn't afford to apologize for Char, where she might overhear and contradict him. But . . .

"Beth," he managed at last, "are you all right?"

"She's fine." Nalani pushed herself forward, blocking his view. She crossed her arms over her dark sweater and glared at him as if the encounter with Charla was his fault.

There came a loud rapid-fire honking.

"Oh my God, man!" Tosa was shouting.

Salva's attention finally turned. And landed on a bright yellow sports car with a lowered convertible hood.

Pepe leaped out over the front driver's-side door and landed in front of Char. "Care for a ride, my lady?" he said.

Her hand slid to Pepe's chest as if she had to hold on to him in order to stay upright.

His grip closed around her fingers, then pulled her toward the passenger's side.

"Holy Swiss cheese!" Tosa hopped into the back without an escort. "Get out. Just get outta here!" He raised his hands toward the fog. "Your mom's seriously lettin' you drive this thing?!"

"What does she have to say about it?" Pepe scoffed. "It was her parents who bought it."

"Man, I could work three shifts at the machine shop and not be able to afford the insurance on this baby." Tosa looked up. "Well, Salva, you gonna stand there all night or get in?"

"He's speechless," Pepe teased. "His Highness is so blown away by this beauty's excellence that he's frozen to that field, and we'll have to thaw him out next spring."

Right. Salva glanced back toward Beth. But she had

disappeared. Along with Nalani and Luka. No doubt they'd finally headed for the dance.

"Come on, Resendez!" Pepe climbed into the driver's seat. "Who's stalling now? The later we show for Linette's party, the harder time Tosa's gonna have gaining her attention."

Tosa didn't look too concerned. He was pounding the top of the door. "You know how many horses this baby has?"

Salva approached, then looked directly down at him and admitted ignorance. "Nope."

"We are talkin' *three hundred horsepower*, man. *Trescientos*."

"Well, move aside." Salva swung one leg, then the other, over the door and slid down onto the black leather. He closed his eyes and breathed the incredible smell. *En el nombre de Dios.* Life was unfair, and sometimes that wasn't a bad thing.

The car screeched away from the curb, wrapped its way around the field, and headed for the party.

It was possible, he realized about an hour later, as the music blared from Linette's family room stereo, that he might have made an error in judgment—by suggesting Pepe go after Char. Not that Salva wanted her. One thing he was not feeling, as he watched her wind her arms and legs around his best friend, then down one beer after another, was jealousy.

"Hey, Tos." Salva leaned on the back of the chair where his friend was sprawled, happily losing at poker. "You think maybe you could tell Pepe to ease up a little on the charm? He doesn't need to get her plastered, you know?"

Char was a slow learner, though a lot of Salva's peers weren't aware of it because nobody's stereotype of someone with a learning disability was a gorgeous girl with bare shoulders and legs that stretched to heaven. But he knew she didn't like to admit when there was something she didn't understand.

And she would not have understood his rejection.

He had told her to shut up. She would comprehend that—would have taken it hard. Would have grasped, finally, that their relationship wasn't going to the next level.

But she wouldn't understand why. Not really. And he couldn't explain—couldn't apologize for shooting her down in public because she might misinterpret the apology as an expression of interest. Which would leave him right back where he had started.

Of course, she wasn't *acting* hurt. Laughing at his best friend's jokes and accepting every drink Pepe passed her way. She was acting as though the evening's outcome was just as she'd expected.

Tosa glanced up from his cards for the first time since their blond hostess had waved him aside and disappeared into the ranks of her other guests—a diss that might not have been a bad thing. Salva wasn't sure his openhearted friend was any more prepared to function at Linette's speed than Char was at Pepe's.

"I don't think it's Pepe's fault," Tosa said. "She was drinking plenty at Linette's last party all on her own."

Probably true. Char did struggle with setting her own

boundaries, never having had any practice. "Yeah, well," Salva stated, "Pepe doesn't have to help her down that road, does he?"

"Listen, man," Tosa replied, "I'm not getting in his way tonight. That girl hasn't given him the time of day before, and I don't think he's gonna be too happy if we interrupt. If you want to play hero, go right ahead."

"I can't. You know he'd read it the wrong way." *As would Char.*

Tosa took a swig of his own drink. "You sure about that?"

"Yes."

"Cuz there are plenty of other girls lookin', if you're on the prowl."

Salva was *not* on the prowl, though it was easier to worry about Pepe and Char's relationship than to analyze his own status. "I'm not really looking."

Tosa wiggled his eyebrows, then shrugged. "Well, you probably don't have to look, the way you smell in that cologne. You friggin' reek of desperation."

Salva put him in a headlock.

Never a good idea with a guy over six feet tall.

In a matter of seconds, Tosa had him on the floor, one foot on Salva's back. "Footrest for sale! Anybody want a footrest?"

Salva swept his friend's ankle, then rolled. And Tosa crashed down beside him. They both broke into wild laughter.

Which finally brought their blond hostess back into the room. "Listen, you two," she snapped, "anyone who breaks furniture in this house has to work it off, and you don't wanta know what kind of trashy jobs my stepmom comes up with."

Tosa sobered, giving her his largest puppy-dog eyes. "Sorry, Linette."

She bought it. Salva could see the witch-in-charge go right out of her and the maybe-I-should-take-another-look seduction slide into her features. A second later, the duo was winding its way into the next room.

Great. Well, that had worked well. Now Salva had not only one friend seducing a girl who was two speeds behind him, but a second friend getting seduced.

Which was what parties were all about.

So why am I not looking for someone to lock lips with? Just for entertainment's sake? Salva let his gaze travel slowly around the room. There were three, maybe four unattached girls here who weren't hideous. But he just couldn't see taking the trouble.

He dropped down into Tosa's vacated chair beside the poker table. The guys there were playing for chips. Literally. Nacho Cheese and Sour Cream and Onion.

"You want in?" the dealer asked.

"Naw." Salva leaned back and stared up at the ceiling fan.

He couldn't concentrate.

Kept having the same vision over and over in his head. And he couldn't seem to clear it. What he saw—what he kept seeing, as the blades of the fan spun above him, were the auburn highlights in Beth's hair. And the doelike eyes that had stared up at him from her ghostly face. And the way that white dress had draped her slender frame.

The night was insane. He must be high on adrenaline. The game had been incredible. The car was—face it, the car was unlike anything he'd ever planned on riding in during his life. And as designated driver, he was going to get to drive it home.

But really, he wasn't even thinking about that drive.

Because he couldn't get rid of the realization that had rocked and cracked his world like a broken windshield. Just before the car had pulled up.

She might be crazy—wearing that thin dress on a night that was maybe twenty-nine degrees. And she might be a nerd—because, really, who from Liberty High School ever applied to go to Stanford? And she was most definitely a walking disaster area.

But she was also *beautiful*.

8

THE DARE

The minute hand on the multipurpose room clock clicked to twenty past, and Beth felt the sharp movement as though it were a scalpel at her throat. The same scalpel that had sliced through her on homecoming night and continued to cut deeper during the long walk home in the dark. Alone. To the empty trailer.

Her mother's constant absence and Ni's newfound distractedness should have accustomed Beth to being stood up. She clenched the frayed strap of her backpack and forced herself to rise from the stage. *He isn't coming.*

For the two weeks since that awful night when Char's comment had ripped the scab off Beth's grief, Salva had had no time for study sessions, due to extra sports practice. Then this weekend, she had seen the writing, not on the wall but in full-color print on the front page of the regional paper. State champions. And his picture—of course it had been *his* picture—

along with the words *brilliant* and *all-star*. The town had thrown a five-star parade.

What did she expect—that he would remember her paltry little tutoring sessions after all that? Hardly. He had passed his first term in English. It wasn't a stellar mark. He should want to achieve more. But there was no point watching the scalpel of time until it bled her dry.

She vacated the room for the hall. Shouts from JV basketball practice echoed from the gym around the corner as she strode in the opposite direction. The wing was dark, except for the light from cit/gov, aka Coach Robson's room. And the green glow of the nearest exit.

Just go home, she told herself. *Go home and finish that essay for the Ag Association on why you want to be a famous writer and why they should choose to invest a thousand dollars in you even though you never want to look up the rear end of a cow, create a strain of lettuce, or cure onion blight. Go home and forget about him.*

Forget she'd ever dreamed. Her head shrilled at the thought.

It took a moment to realize the sound—a high-pitched electronic buzz—was actually coming from cit/gov.

She glanced into the room.

And found Salva. Asleep. Slumped on a keyboard, arms folded, head sideways, eyes closed. Oblivious to the buzzing keys.

Unwanted empathy rushed to her chest. The screen was a deep liquid blue. Either he'd finished what he was writing, or he'd lost the document. Her gaze flicked to the printer.

CHAPTER 5: WITHOUT PRECEDENT. He had typed up his notes for tomorrow's cit/gov test. *Who did that?*

She turned off the Power button on the outlet.

Peace reigned as he continued to sleep. He looked younger. Innocent. Dark eyelashes rested low. Her hand hovered above his face, so near she could touch that stray strand of hair on his forehead. Perhaps he hadn't meant to skip the tutoring session after all. He was still at the school, just asleep.

His profile shifted.

And she had the sudden urge to kiss him.

She struggled to suppress the instinct, but her face lowered.

The eyelashes flicked up, and she was close, *way* too close. He looked startled. Trapped.

Her hand brushed his rising shoulder in her attempt to pull away. "Y-you fell asleep." She staggered back.

He sat erect, then exhaled and ran his fingers through his hair. "Sorry." He glanced at his wrist, seemed to realize his watch wasn't there, and squinted up at the clock. "The computer lab was closed for some reason. Coach Robson said I could type here." He gave a quick glance toward the printer. "I must have crashed. I . . . haven't gotten a lot of sleep in the last couple weeks."

She hadn't slept too well either, since homecoming. Since *he* had defended *her*. Though she'd been trying in her pathetic hopeless way to forget about that moment. To remember that he hadn't even noticed her at first, hanging in the background by the bleachers, and when she'd finally gathered enough courage to congratulate him, he'd stared at her like he'd never seen her before. And then Char—

Beth felt her stomach clench.

He had probably forgotten about the entire confrontation.

"Listen . . ." Salva made a fist and ran his knuckles along the table's edge. "I've been meaning . . . that is . . . I wanted to apologize for Char. For what she said to you after the homecoming game."

Beth's heart stumbled.

"She didn't know"—he kept talking—"at least, I don't think she knows . . . about your grandmother. Though even if she knew, she wouldn't understand." There was something in his voice—something that chimed in unison with Beth's own sense of isolation.

"But you do," Beth whispered. "Don't you, Salva?"

He pushed his chair back from the keyboard, plucked the notes from the printer, and walked away, cutting through the five rows of desks. Then he dug his hands into his pockets and stared out the window into the early November night. The end of daylight saving time had rendered the Earth dark.

Silence filled the separation.

She wanted to offer him solace—the same gift he had given her the day he had fixed all the zippers on her backpack. "Salva, if you ever want to talk—"

"It's getting late." He cut her off, his gaze still toward the glass.

She swallowed the rejection. "If you want to postpone our session—"

"No!" He spun, strode to the back of the room, and began pacing between the signs UNCLE SAM WANTS YOU and HELL NO, WE WON'T GO on Robson's time line of political quotes. "I can't fall any further behind. We've got a cit/gov test tomorrow, an AP lit quiz on Thursday, and a paper due in career prep. Plus, I have to work extra hours to make up for what I missed during the championship. And we have our second round of SATs this weekend."

She blinked at the panic in his voice, then stated the obvious. "Yes, but you test well." He may have been afraid of automatic toilets back in elementary school, but he had also been the first kid to pass his time tests, the kid with the most stickers on the class chart, the kid whose name was *always* called when the teacher read off the super-high exam scores for the display board. *In fact* . . . Beth scanned the corkboard above the computers. Sure enough, Salva's chapter 4 exam was posted at the center.

He paused at THE BUCK STOPS HERE. "You must have done pretty well last spring if you're planning to go to Stanford."

With most people it would have felt like bragging to share her first-round SAT scores. But not with him. She told him what she'd earned. "What about you?" she challenged, stepping closer, certain he had at least a fifty-point advantage.

He displayed a sudden interest in the ceiling map of the world. And told her.

Her mouth dropped open. That was more like a hundred points. "Where are *you* applying?" she asked.

His eyes remained on the map as he reeled off the names of six colleges, all within the state.

Ridiculous. "You could get into those even with a D in AP English," she said.

"I need scholarships."

"Give me a break, Salva." She snatched the notes from his hand. "You should be aiming Ivy League."

He dropped the feigned interest in the ceiling map, doubt plain on his face. "It's not that easy," he said.

Easy? "You could go to Princeton. Or Harvard. Or UPenn. You have the grades and the student involvement." Maybe he couldn't afford to spend a year in Kenya helping the needy, but he had plenty of qualifications. So what was the barrier?

He reached for his notes.

She held them beyond his grasp. "I dare you." The words sprang forth without intention. "I dare you to apply to three top-ten colleges and see if you get in."

He veered around her, retreated toward the darkened computer, and lifted a folder.

Was he just going to let his future coast? How could he push himself so far and then stop?

She approached slowly. "Salva?"

He whirled and snagged the notes from her hand. "Okay," he said. "*If* you'll partner me on my Shakespeare project."

She staggered back. "W-we don't even start Shakespeare until January," she said.

He filed the notes in the folder. "Yes, but I might not have anything to hold over your head then. And where else am I going to find an expert who's actually in drama?"

Electricity ran straight through her gut. *Get a grip, Beth.*

The Mercenary's Shakespeare projects were notorious. Students had to read at least three plays, pass a killer exam, and then pick a scene to perform in public for maximum impact.

"Look," he continued, "we're graded based on the impression we make on the student body. What is the chance you'll make as much impact by yourself as with me?"

No chance. All he had to do was lift his pinky finger to get everyone's attention.

Half an hour ago, she'd thought this was over—that she'd never spend another minute alone with him. And now he was asking—no, daring—her to make a commitment that ran through March. She was in this far too deep. "You'll fill out three full applications to Ivy League colleges?"

He nodded.

"And you'll post them before deadline?"

He rolled his eyes but concurred. "As long as I pick the place and time of the performance. Do we have a dare?"

"You have to show me the applications first."

"Do we have a *dare*?" Those eyes were very dark, her own personal abyss.

She had never been so thrilled to drown. "Yes."

9

¿QUÉ ES?

Harvard. Princeton. Yale. Salva tried not to wince as the woman behind the post office counter pounded the stamp—once, twice, thrice—and tossed the applications onto a pile behind her. She slammed the metal window down in his face. It was already five minutes after five o'clock, and the December night had coiled into darkness. He had been the last at the end of a long line.

Salva turned and shoved his way into the cold—the kind of cold that made his ears curl and his teeth ache. No snow— just the bitter chill and expanding patches of ice. He buried his hands in his sleeves and hugged his arms to his chest, an action that rendered no more defense than his thin jacket.

The idea of spending the night at the Laundromat was unbearable.

He'd thought about bailing on the post office trip, but then he would have had to relive the interrogation he had faced this morning. *"¿Salva, qué es?"* Talia had asked as he'd set the first of the envelopes on top of his school gear.

"*Sí*, Salva, what are you mailing?" Casandra had chimed in.

"They're nothing," he'd said, brushing off the question.

Nothing, he repeated to himself now. *Forget about the applications.* They were just a dare, and he'd lived up to his side, which was the point—so he didn't flunk AP English.

And he wasn't flunking. With Beth's help, he'd pulled up his grade to almost a B.

She'd even told him this afternoon that his final college essays were "awesome."

Bizarre. Because Beth didn't use the term *awesome* with regard to his writing. At least, she never had before. She wasn't as harsh now as back in September, but she used lots of phrases like "I think you could make this stronger" and "Get to the point," her polite version of "Cut the crap."

What did "awesome" mean? That after four revisions, it was obvious his essays were so bad he hadn't a hope of ever fixing them to a level that would gain him acceptance?

Of course I won't get accepted. People from Podunk don't get into top-ten colleges.

But he couldn't tell Beth that. She seemed so certain she was going to Stanford; and if she was going to be crushed, he didn't want to be on the side of I-told-you-so.

Though maybe he was wrong. Maybe she *would* get in. She'd claimed her grandfather was an alum. Expensive schools counted things like that. They called them Legacy Rules or something.

Salva, on the other hand, had a father who had become a U.S. citizen less than two years ago—not exactly a legacy.

And a mother who is dead. Memories from the hospital threatened: *Mamá's* voice, faint from the pain; her skin, bruised purple around the central line in her neck; her eyes, glazing over as the nurse had pumped in more medication. The caustic complaint of the old man in the waiting room who had claimed that *these people* were the reason no one could afford insurance.

Salva's feet skidded on ice. He grabbed hold of a slumped fence, managed to regain his footing, and looked up.

To his surprise, light glowed from the single wide. *What the H?*

Had Char dropped off Talia and Casandra at home early with no one here to watch them?

He bolted forward through the gate, slid again, and grabbed the handrail, then hauled himself up the porch, tugged open the door, and braved the Shrine—careful to keep his eyes off the portrait on the living room wall.

"*¡Salva, finalmente está!*" Casandra barreled into him. "He's here. He's here! *¡A cenar!*"

Talia arrived, and they dragged him into the kitchen.

Where the smell of *Mamá's* tamales punched him in the gut: chicken, *queso blanco*, chilies, and the overwhelming scent of homemade corn *masa*. An intense longing seared through his chest, and he fought for control. Losing.

His older sister stood behind the table. Her black hair, a foot shorter than *Mamá's*, was pushed back in a straightforward ponytail. She wore an apron over her shirt, and her forehead was frosted with sweat, or perhaps steam, as she wielded a simple kitchen knife with the speed of a cook who'd paid her dues in a Mexican restaurant. A pile of minced tomatoes covered the cutting board.

"¡Todavía no!" She swatted Casandra's pointing finger away from the nearby pan of rolled corn husks, then covered them over with a towel. "The salad isn't ready yet, so unless you want to help . . ."

His younger sisters hightailed it.

Salva scowled. "Lucia, what are you doing here? It's the week before your finals."

She was supposed to be two hours away, studying her ass off at the local community college. Her grades hadn't been so hot last quarter.

She handed over a metal bowl and a head of romaine lettuce. "I did the laundry. Shred that."

"Papá will lose it if he finds you here in the middle of the week."

"No te preocupes. His shift's not over till ten. I'll be long gone, and then I'll pass my finals before coming home for Christmas." She pushed aside the tomatoes and removed the stem from a yellow pepper. "What were you *not* doing here?"

Like it was any of her business. But Lucia's opinion had

always had more influence over Salva than he cared to admit. Even his *name*. It was her fault he was called Salva, instead of the common and more masculine Salvino, because when Lucia was two, she'd thought everyone's name should end with an *a*—*Papá*, *Mamá*, and *Salva*. Only his older brother, Miguel, had escaped.

"Salva," she continued to pry, "why are you so late?"

It was a Tuesday, which wasn't much of an excuse. The deal with Char was supposed to be on an as-needed basis, but he had needed to submit the applications. And Beth had agreed to stay after school today to look at them one last time.

He thought about trying to explain but could already hear Lucia's response. *So you could live up to a dare? Is that more important than your sisters?*

It wasn't. He knew it wasn't. His mother would never have been okay with the whole arrangement with Char. And clearly, Lucia wasn't either.

She finished chopping up the yellow pepper. "I thought you were supposed to be home earlier now," she said, reaching for the half-filled bowl of lettuce. There was a brief tug-of-war over the bowl, which she won. "Since you're free of all your celebrity football engagements." She cracked a smile.

He couldn't help grinning. He knew she'd read every press article about the team.

She swiped the chopped-up pepper and tomatoes into the salad.

He snagged a large spoon from a drawer and held it out to her, yanked it away, then offered it back. And lost it.

"Where *were* you?" she repeated the question as she tossed the vegetables.

"School," he replied. "Someone was helping me with homework."

The spoon clattered against the side of the bowl. "What's her name?"

¡Ay! Too late, he realized his mistake. If he'd told her he was working with a friend, she wouldn't have thought much of it, but his *friends* typically needed Salva's help, not the other way around. "Look, we have a project together," he said. Though, technically, the project hadn't started yet, but he didn't want her getting the wrong idea about Beth.

Which would be what, exactly?

He'd spent more time than was necessary over the past month studying the shade of his study partner's hair in different angles of light. During those two weeks before the state championship, he'd almost convinced himself that his sudden attraction to her on homecoming was a complete deviation. That Char's comment had instigated some kind of gut reaction to defend Beth as a victim. And totally skewed his view of reality.

In class, he'd seen nothing but the walking disaster area. Same mess. Same common brown eyes and frizz. And then he'd woken up that one day after school to find her, inches away, staring at him with those wide doe's eyes and that rare glitter of red in her hair.

Salva had almost bolted. Yet ten minutes later he had found himself in the middle of a stupid, commitment-filled dare.

Which was *none* of his older sister's business.

"Casandra! Talia!" he called, "*¡A cenar!*"

The pounding of feet answered.

Lucia crumbled the *queso fresco* over the top of the salad. "Poorly done, *hermano*." She gave him a look that turned serious. "And here I thought it was just *Mamá* you wouldn't talk about."

He opened the fridge, took out the milk, and closed the door with more force than was necessary. They weren't doing this.

His younger sisters arrived, talking over each other.

"You'll never believe—"

"Guess what happened today!"

He let the nine-year-old voices drown out the anger he didn't have a right to feel.

The dinner discussion was all girl stuff. If only Miguel would move back to balance things out, but after three and a half years, that wasn't going to happen. Salva should have known, maybe, from the beginning, considering the circumstances. The fights between his older brother and *Papá*. And everything Miguel had had to give up for *la familia*.

He had been Salva's hero, their parents' pride. The first child to graduate—to get accepted into college. *El futuro, Papá* had called him. A future sucked into the swirling pit of hospital and funeral bills. Miguel had given up everything—his tuition, school, an entire year of his life—to work and take care of *la familia.*

And then the fights had started: *Papá* ordering Miguel to go back to school; Miguel arguing that there wasn't any money; *Papá* in denial, trying to fulfill the promise he had made to his wife that all her children would get an education—slamming that shredded, impossible dream into his oldest son's chest, pushing Miguel away when the last thing any of them could afford to lose was another family member.

The entire year had been like a chasm.

Salva felt his stomach roll backward as he took a bite of his mother's tamales. *I can't eat this.*

He stood.

Then froze as his father walked in.

"*¡Papá!*" the younger girls shouted. "You're home early!"

Salva's gaze shot toward Lucia.

She didn't raise an eyebrow, though she must have been stunned. Instead, she pushed the tamales toward the empty plate she had set out for whenever *Papá* came home. "*¿A cenar?*" she asked.

"*Claro.*" Señor Resendez made a great show of inhaling the aroma, then seated himself. He swallowed his first tamale in three bites. "Sit down, Salvador."

Salva sat.

And watched as his father bit into his next *masa* wrap.

"Storm is coming," the older man said. "We had to shut down the plant. I do not think you will be able to return to school tomorrow, Lucita."

"*Está bien*," she replied.

It wasn't *bien*, but Salva had to hand it to his sister. She wasn't the type to freak in the face of an impending lecture.

Papá had a gift with people. Everyone liked him: the neighbors, the workers at the plant, the owners who had made him manager. Señor Resendez was open, friendly—the type of person who could make a perfect stranger spill the details of his or her life in a matter a minutes. He had a reputation for being a guy who'd laugh off your mistakes, get you out of a mess, and charge nothing but his own pleasure in retelling the story.

Unless you happened to be one of his own children.

In which case, you'd better succeed.

Their father finished his third tamale, then started in on his favorite topic. "So what did you learn today?"

Casandra and Talia reeled off a song with all the state capitals in it. Both girls were graced with praise.

"And you, Salva?" Señor Resendez started his fourth tamale.

Salva hadn't learned much. With all the random Christmas stuff—the b-ball tournament, winter concert, drama production—academics at the high school had pretty much crumbled to a halt. He told about the food bank drive he was running through ASB.

"*Sí, bien.*" *Papá* took a drink of water, then finally turned his attention to Lucia. "And what are you doing home before finals, Lucita?" He set down his glass. "Did your power go out again?"

That was the excuse she had tried last time.

"I didn't have class this afternoon." She lowered her own glass.

"And now you will not be back for class in the morning. You will not gain a transfer into a four-year college with bad grades, Lucita."

She sat perfectly still, meeting his eyes, then said, "I don't need a four-year degree."

My God. Had she learned nothing from Miguel's experience?

Lucia continued, "I can get my certification to give meds right now, and as soon as I graduate, I can extend my hours at the local retirement home."

"That is *nada.*" Señor Resendez brushed off the statement as if she hadn't even bothered to talk.

"It's a good job," she said.

"There is no future there. Your mother and I, we bring you here so you can get an education. This is all that matters."

"Really?" she snapped back. "What about *la familia*? I picked the girls up from school and spent the last two hours with them. Why don't you ask Salva why he wasn't here until after five?" She torqued the conversation.

No way. Salva didn't know why she was pushing this argument. As he saw it, she was lucky *Papá* wasn't taking her seriously. It was lousy timing on her part. Or maybe not. Maybe the tamales were part of the plan. But Salva wasn't taking this hit for her. *She* didn't have to live here. "I was at school," he said, "*studying.*"

Which was a lie.

"Is there something I should know, Salvador?" His father's voice was calm, the tone used when expecting a truthful answer. If there was anything more important to *Papá* than education, it was honesty.

Salva felt his throat tighten. He could tell his father about the Ivy League applications, but what would be the point? Deep down, Salva kind of wanted to know if he could get in. Just for the sake of knowing. But even if he won every local five-hundred and thousand-dollar scholarship, he couldn't afford one of those schools. And *Papá* didn't need to feel bad about not being able to send his son anywhere he wanted to go. Plus, there was no point having the whole what-do-you-mean-you-want-to-move-to-the-East-Coast argument.

"No," Salva answered his father, then took a bite of the salad and almost wept. *Jesús Cristo.* The peppers were hot.

Winter featured snow, freezing rain, and three months of cold wind that would have stripped the wings off every butterfly in Salva's birth state of Michoacán. Then March rolled in with a pile of ditched snow tires and the mingled odors of solvent, oil, and grease.

Salva sat on a stack of new tires in the machine shop. The place had an overflow of work. Which meant Tosa had had to come in to help his old man even on a Sunday afternoon. And Pepe had magnanimously decided he and his best friend should go along. To provide a distraction.

Fortunately, the owner almost never stuck his head out of the office. And Tosa's father, who was out back most of the time anyway, didn't have enough English to follow the shop talk. "So what's the deal with the blonde?" Pepe asked, leaning casually against a busted-up fender. He flicked a string of aluminum bottle tops at Tosa, who was defenseless on a creeper under a dented-up Chevy. "Any action yet?"

In Pepe's vocab, action required all four bases.

Metal clanged from under the car, followed by soft swearing and a squeal as the rollers of the creeper shifted. "We're off for the moment," Tosa said.

"Man, you weren't ever on." Pepe smirked.

Tosa's hand came out from under the vehicle and patted the ground, about a foot from a half-inch wrench. Salva got up and handed over the tool, then went back to his perch.

"What about you, Real?" The question shot from under the Chevy. "You're the one with the steady girlfriend." There came the sound of metal screeching against the floor.

Salva cringed. After all the years he'd spent as Char's protector, he wasn't too keen on hearing about his best friend's exploits with her.

Pepe lifted a bad bolt from the discard can. "Yeah, well, we aren't wasting our time. It'd be a hell of a lot easier, though, if Mr. Super Genius over here"—he chucked the bolt in Salva's direction—"didn't keep leaving his little sisters at the place for Char to babysit."

Salva caught the bolt and flung it back. There better *not* be any action while his sisters were over there.

"Speakin' of whom," Pepe added, "what's up with you, Resendez? I ain't seen you with a chick all winter. You turnin' into the pope or something?"

Salva knew his dearth of a sex life was crazy. He hadn't been dateless for this long since he'd entered Liberty High, but—

well, he kept having dreams about the wrong girl.

Tosa rolled out from under the Chevy and chucked a half-dozen bottle caps back at Pepe. "Better watch yourself, Real! You wouldn't want to wind up stuck here with Charla while Resendez cleans up all the college girls next fall."

Salva grinned and tossed his tall friend a water bottle. "You mean, *both* you and I clean them up; right, Tos?"

"Nah." Tosa unscrewed the lid and gulped about half the contents of the bottle, then stared down into it. "I'm not going to college."

"What?" Pepe came off the fender.

"Um . . ." Tosa screwed on the bottle lid, then unscrewed it again. "I'm thinkin' maybe the army."

A hail of bolts fell from Pepe's fingers. "What the H would you wanta do that for?"

Salva didn't care much for the idea either—the thought of his big, easygoing friend killing someone. But then—short of a trade school, which there was no way Tosa's family was going to be able to afford—the military was a real option.

The tall guy looked up at Salva as if for approval. "Well, it'd be easier, you know."

Meaning the whole citizenship process. There was no way either of Tosa's parents was going to pass the English test before he turned eighteen. Though, as Salva saw it, there were a heck of a lot better ways to become a citizen than to get yourself killed. But he didn't have a right to talk. His father had passed the test two years ago, and Salva didn't have to deal with the whole visa mess. *Lucky.* He knew that. Just one more thing he owed *Papá*, because Salva never could have applied for the same scholarships if he'd had to fill in the wrong bubble on all those forms.

He slid off the tires and clapped Tosa on the back. "The army'd be lucky to have you."

"What's that supposed to mean?" Pepe demanded.

Salva knew his best friend was still under the illusion the three of them were going to spend the next four years together. Which wasn't going to happen. No way Tosa would have gotten into a better school than Community. And Salva had already received a yes from Regional at least, not that Regional was at the top of his list.

He and Pepe needed to talk.

But not here. And not now. What was needed now was action.

"It means," Salva said, "I bet they could use a half-decent mechanic." He glanced around behind him. No sign of the shop owner. Or Tosa's father. "Especially one we've primed so well for battle, don't you think?" Salva picked up a grease rag, wadded it tight, and hurled it at Pepe.

"Oh, man," Pepe said, ducking the rag and crouching down behind the busted fender, "are you sure you wanta go there?"

"Definitely," Tosa answered instead, snagging the box of remaining rags and dodging behind the fresh stack of tires.

Which meant Salva had to dive for cover behind the cabinet by the open office door.

"Incoming!" Pepe shouted, and what followed was a barrage: aluminum cans, bottle tops, rags, the empty water bottle, a container of glue, lubricant. The rules were simple. No nuts, bolts, or wrenches. Nothing that would leave a hole in your head. And when you ran out of stuff to throw, you were out.

Salva gave up first. The other guys, closer to each other, kept trading ammo.

During a brief lull in the combat, he heard the customer bell ring and moved to close the door, but he paused as he caught sight of the hopeless look on Tosa's father's face. The owner, who should have been manning the desk, must have slacked off early. Salva stepped through the doorway and shut out the sounds of renewed warfare.

Señor Tosa was the inverse of his son, nearly as tall but scary skinny and a total introvert. He was also a brilliant mechanic. But no way was he going to be able to follow the diatribe being flung at him from the guy who'd just entered the shop.

The customer, a white guy maybe in his thirties, though it was hard to tell under the patchy facial hair, railed away about his Jeep losing horsepower. The damn thing had been running fine, he claimed, when he'd got it two months ago. He plucked at his tight T-shirt, not a good look on a guy with a gut, then slammed his chewed-up baseball cap down on the counter and demanded a quote.

"En-engine no work." Señor Tosa glanced nervously toward the yellow invoices by the hat.

"What the hell you think I've been sayin'?" The customer spat a wad of chew onto the floor.

Real classy. "Just a sec," Salva said to the jerk, then turned and did his best to translate the problem without wasting his breath.

"Change oil?" Señor Tosa asked.

The customer was turning purple. "What do I look like, some teenager?"

I'm guessing you've trashed a lot more vehicles than I have.

"Air filter?" asked Tosa's father.

The guy scoffed and hitched his thumbs through his belt loops.

Señor Tosa dropped into Spanish.

"If the air filter was installed incorrectly," Salva translated, "the dirt might come straight in and damage the engine."

The customer folded his arms over his chest. "I don't wanta know what this grease rag"—he jerked his head at Señor Tosa—"thinks I might've done wrong; I wanta know what he's gonna do to fix the problem. And how much it's gonna cost me."

How about some time in anger management? Or maybe with an antibiotic. A circle on the guy's arm looked suspiciously like ringworm.

Señor Tosa explained that he would have to check out the engine first.

"So you're saying you can't do your job?" the other man griped.

Salva wished he could send a silent message to the mechanic. *Just let him take his beer gut somewhere else and see how fast he gets a quote on a Sunday.*

Señor Tosa, his face blank, asked for the man's phone number, promising to call back with the quote by four o'clock.

The customer seemed to get over himself long enough to reel off his number, which Salva scribbled down on one of the yellow invoices.

The guy swiped up his hat and stomped toward the door.

"We'll need the keys," Salva called after him.

The man spat again. Then he dug into his jeans pocket, pulled out an object, and sent it spiraling in a lousy throw. Salva caught the key.

"You tell your real boss," the guy said to him, "I'm talkin' to someone who speaks *English* on the phone, not this Spanish flunky. This is America."

And the guy walked out.

Salva still hadn't gotten the anger out of his head by the next afternoon as he entered the cardboard forest that now filled the multipurpose room. Rows of wooden stands with corrugated tree trunks and boughs covered in paper leaves stood in his way. He burst past one, knocked it down, and sent dozens of leaves blowing in every direction.

"Careful!" Beth gasped from the stage. "That's the forest for the spring production. They're not dry."

Yeah, well, he'd figured that out a little late.

He reached for the sundered foliage and got his palm covered in glue. *Ugh!*

Beth came forward with a wet towel and reached for his hand.

He tugged away, grabbing the towel more brusquely than he should have.

"Is something wrong?" she asked.

Yeah, something was wrong. And there wasn't a damn thing he could do about it. Which bugged the hell out of him.

He wiped his hand.

She stood there, just waiting at first, then crouched down and began to pick up the ruined leaves. "What is it?"

She doesn't want to know. No one ever wanted to know. And the people who did know—his father, Señor Tosa, Señora Mendoza—they all preached the same silent mantra. *Poner la otra mejilla.* Sometimes he hated the friggin' Catholic Church!

"Salva?"

"This is America!" The words burst out before he had a clue he was going to say them.

"Oh"—Beth paused in her leaf gathering and grinned up at him—"is it?"

Exactly. "What makes people think I need to hear it?!" He whirled and crossed through a row of drying trees, separating her from his anger. "Or that anyone needs to hear it?"

The tone of her voice sobered. "It's a defense, I guess. For people who are scared."

He kicked the wooden stand of another tree without thinking, then reached out to rescue it. More leaves tumbled. "Of what?" He found it really hard to believe that the jerk at the machine shop had been scared of Tosa's father.

"Of their own ignorance."

The tree trunk was vibrating. *She was right.* He knew she was right, though he'd never heard anyone put it that way before.

"Who said it?" she asked.

And the vibrating stopped. He realized he didn't even know the name of the idiot.

Sighing, Salva bent down to pick up the mess.

She eased a garbage can, already half filled with discarded leaves, in his direction. "Tell me."

"You don't want to hear about it."

"I wouldn't ask if I didn't."

He stared at her. His mother had been like that. She'd never asked a question without wanting to know the answer. Beth— well—he didn't have to impress her. And she didn't come with all the baggage that was in his family. Plus, nothing was too "out there" or "over her head." Or too deep. She seemed to operate on a plane of feeling.

Salva stretched for a distant leaf, then found himself spilling: the details of the conversation in the machine shop, the thousand other times he'd heard that stupid comment about

America, and all his own logical arguments against it—that *America* included Latin America, that English was the native language of England, that no one who'd never learned a second language had the right to judge.

"You're right," Beth said when he was done. No arguments. Or vacillations.

He felt like he could breathe for the first time all day.

She was silent for maybe a minute, then asked, "Have you read "Ending Poem" by Rosario Morales and Aurora Levins Morales?"

Random. He wiped up the floor with the wet towel.

"It's by Puerto Rican writers," she continued, "about celebrating all the cultures that make us who we are. It's kind of awesome."

Which was so Beth. Telling him to read a poem. As if real people could just work out all their problems through literature. Like the characters in a book.

Well, maybe not in the plays he'd been reading for AP English: *Hamlet, Julius Caesar, Othello.* Salva stood up and draped the soiled towel over the edge of the water fountain. Sometimes heroes didn't solve anything. Sometimes they died.

11

REHEARSAL

The young man in front of Beth, his hair tousled, shirt loose, taking out his vengeance on paper trees, was not the Salva she knew. Though she'd had fair warning. He had slammed his locker door, loudly, between first and second period. And *everyone* had stared.

"Looks like something's blown the god's cool," Ni had joked at the time.

But Beth had been too consumed with disguising her own automatic desire to defend him to pay much heed. She knew Ni's sarcasm came from a history of defending *her* after spending hours, in the eighth-grade girls' bathroom, watching Beth cry her eyes out over Salva's failure to notice her. Which was why Beth had failed to tell her best friend about the study sessions. For five and a half months.

I should have been up front from the very beginning.

There was so much about Salva that Beth wanted to discuss.

His mother for one. He *never* spoke about her.

In fact, he rarely talked about anyone in his family, though Beth remembered he had an older brother who had picked him up every day from elementary school. And she knew Salva also had three sisters, the eldest of whom, Lucia, had graduated from Liberty two years ago. And about whom, when asked if he saw her often, he'd replied, "Too often."

As for his younger sisters, he claimed they drove him batty, but Beth could tell he cared about them because he had bailed on her only twice this winter—once to see their music concert and once to pick up Talia when she had been sick.

He didn't talk about his father either, but in the essay for Yale, in which the applicant had had to select a hero, he had chosen "*Papá*," whom Salva seemed to think had built the entire world with his own hands, then schmoozed God into taking the credit. *La familia* obviously meant a lot.

Though perhaps not as much as friendship. Beth had made the error—once—during a study session, of deriding Pepe Real for a brainless comment the guy had made in cit/gov. And Salva had unloaded on her fifty reasons why his best friend was awesome. The whole bond-between-guys-who-could-throw-a-ball escaped her. But she got that her study partner was defending his best friend.

Like Ni had been this morning.

And Ni had been right about Salva losing his cool. Beth had never seen him rail about anything as passionately as he had during the last few minutes. Or—she glanced up at the clock—the past half hour. "Umm . . . I hate to mention it," she said, "but sign-ups are tomorrow. We have to choose a Shakespeare scene or . . . risk dire consequences from the Mercenary."

Their teacher had spent the morning's lit class stressing the significance of the word *deadline*. "You *will* submit your scene on time," she had declared, "or someone else will have the right to it. You *will* submit your first choice for the location of your performance, or there will be no way to make arrangements. You *will* submit the time of that performance, or you will not go on my schedule. And if you are not on *my* schedule, even if you have the most impressive project in Liberty High history, you will *still* fail."

Salva looked up at Beth with shadowed eyes, but he must have remembered the lecture. He shoved his hands in his pockets and strode past her toward the stage—which she had covered, literally, with copies of every Shakespeare play she'd ever seen or read. Twenty-eight plays. Perhaps too many. But they were really all excellent. And she'd been *trying* to be organized.

He vaulted into the center of the books, then turned in a slow circle, something like a smile creeping onto his face.

"Of course," she said, "if there's a play you'd rather use that's not up there—"

That was definitely a smile. "No offense," he replied, picking up a copy of *Coriolanus* and turning it upside down, "but I think we should do something famous."

Well, he was entitled to an opinion.

"I mean," he added, "we're being graded on the reaction of our audience. And if we do something no one's ever heard of"—his thumb ran through the upside down pages of the play—"they're not gonna get it."

He had a point. She scrambled onto the stage and started picking through the plethora of books. "Okay, well, there's *Hamlet* and *The Taming of the Shrew* and *Henry V,* and—"

"I think we should do *Romeo and Juliet.*"

Henry tumbled from her grasp.

"Cuz, you know," he continued, "it's the only play the freshmen have read."

Her hands were shaking. This couldn't be happening. Could it? She'd been *dreaming* about having the chance to act out the role of Juliet opposite Salva Resendez since freshman lit, when they'd both been chosen to read the balcony scene aloud in class—something she was certain he'd forgotten.

She avoided his gaze, staring instead into the folds of the green curtain gathered at the corner of the stage. "Who . . . who did you want to be?"

"I don't think we should be secondary characters."

She dropped the rest of the books, letting herself believe, for an instant, that this was real.

"But I'm not doing one of those dorky balcony scenes," he said. *So much for the dream.*

"Plus," Salva added, "Romeo is a major pain in the butt for the whole first half of the play. He mopes through the beginning, then falls all over himself for a girl without even *thinking* about the consequences."

Because thought has so much to do with falling in love.

Beth blinked—hard. And had a desperate urge to hide behind the curtain. "So that would leave—"

"The death scene," Salva said.

She wrapped her arms around her chest and gripped her elbows. Did he realize what was in the death scene? "I . . . I suppose we could try—"

"No." He stopped her. "We aren't going to *try* it. We're making a decision and making it work. Right?"

"Um . . ." *Oh my God.* "Right."

"Good, because I have the perfect plan for the venue." He started picking up books.

This couldn't be real. This couldn't be real. This couldn't—

"We had a dare, remember?"

Which meant? She met his gaze at last.

He smoothed his hair and tucked in his shirt. "We're performing in the center of the cafeteria," he said. "At lunchtime. In front of everyone."

The kiss was an issue. Though Salva didn't think it was such a huge one that it merited Beth's pacing the stage at 6:46 A.M. the day of their second rehearsal. The school handbook was pretty clear in its language about "No physical acts of affection on school grounds."

"We could just cut it," he said, leaning back to stare at the tissue-paper-covered stage lights. The line was his, after all. He'd had three million to master in the two days since they'd chosen the scene, in his view much more of an issue. *She'd* set the deadline, an unforeseen consequence of choosing a drama club member as his partner.

"Don't be ridiculous." She swatted him with her script. "You've already learned it."

He quoted at light speed: "'O you the doors of breath, seal with a righteous kiss a dateless bargain to engrossing death.'"

She groaned—no doubt because of his lack of expression. But he'd get to that later, if he could survive waking up at six A.M. three weeks in a row. The scheduling had been a hassle. Beth had insisted, since they had only three weeks to prepare, that they rehearse every day. Which meant he'd had to barter away his Monday and Tuesday evenings so that Char would walk the girls to the morning bus. And that meant he'd spent three hours yesterday at the Laundromat with not only his younger sisters, but also Char's punky nine-year-old brother.

At least Pepe would be happy.

Unlike Beth. Who had begun the morning by forcing Salva to haul a cafeteria-style table onto the stage. And was now harping on the stupid kiss. "The Mercenary said we should cut with *discretion*," she argued. "The line is almost at the end of your speech. It's clearly important."

He rolled over onto his knees and gave her a salute. "All right, madam director, what do you suggest? I could just recite it without any action, but that kind of screams idiot-actor-who-doesn't-know-what-he's-saying, doesn't it?"

She started coiling her pencil in her hair. It was kind of cool seeing her in creative freak-out mode. "Last year," she said, "for the fall drama production, there was a fake kiss behind an umbrella."

"An umbrella in a crypt? Yeah, that sounds good."

She stopped pacing. "You're a great help." Her sarcasm matched his.

And—well—he kind of deserved it. "Look." He stood up, then rotated, his hands facing outward. "The real problem with hiding behind a prop is that we're performing in the center of the cafeteria, so no matter where we try to hide, part of the audience will be able to see."

She pulled her pencil from her hair. "We could move up along a wall—"

"No."

"You are so stubborn!"

This from the girl who'd made him haul a table onto the stage. "Okay, so you're supposed to be dead." He snapped his fingers and pointed her toward the heavy prop. "Go on, die."

She arched her eyebrows, then climbed onto the table and lay back across it horizontally. Her head was still up.

"Dead." He climbed after her in a single movement.

"Actually, I'm not—"

"Sleeping *like* you're dead." He knelt above her.

She dropped her neck back. "Look, Salva, can't you just tell me—"

"Let's assume I'm not kissing you while you're talking."

She shut up.

"Or while I'm still talking," he added. "That gives us a window of four more lines before I drink the poison." *Death by poison in the school cafeteria.* There was a sweet congruity to that. "So maybe I'm just announcing my intention to kiss you and don't try it until after I drink the poison. But then—" He took her shoulders and pulled her close.

She was warm. In his arms.

And smelled like coconut shampoo.

En el nombre de Dios. He dropped her, then reached blindly for his script, pulled it out of his back pocket, and started leafing through it, even though he knew all his lines by heart. The plan had seemed so logical when he had thought it out: the play, the scene, the characters. The words didn't bother him. Lines were just lines. And it was just a project. For a grade.

What he hadn't thought about—what he'd failed to comprehend—was that for the scene to work, he and Beth had to do more than talk.

They had to touch.

"I move close as though I am *going* to kiss you." He avoided her gaze. "But before I actually follow through, the poison kicks in." He grabbed his throat and fell backward on the table. "'Thus with a kiss I die.'"

12

THE SHAKESPEARE PROJECT

Logic sucked, Salva decided, as he stepped into the chaos that was the cafeteria on the day before spring break. Somehow he had survived the three weeks of rehearsals, of listening to his head rather than his body, of telling himself he didn't *feel* anything. Three weeks of waking up from dreams in which he'd succumbed to the smell of coconut and the touch of untamed red-brown hair.

All so he could confront this: banging trays, flying utensils, shouts across the social divide. And the sick smell of scalded vegetables mixed with that of half-burned fried rice. He picked up a tray.

Then cringed as a fortune cookie crunched beneath his shoe.

At least Beth, who had staked out a table at the center of the room, couldn't have witnessed the ill-timed step. She'd been panicking all week over the smallest details: the way her hand should fall as she died, how he should pronounce the word *betossed*, how she should throw the goblet—a school milk carton painted black.

Gossip about the best Shakespeare projects had been up and down the hallway all week. He'd seen two performances personally, one in the gym, and one in the middle of an AP calc quiz. *Now there was an idea. How could your audience not love being interrupted from straining their brains for correct functions by Caliban, Trinculo, and Stephano?*

Though, of course, Salva hadn't needed their help. He'd been phoning in an A in calc all year. The course didn't deserve its reputation.

Unlike AP English. Where a full third of his grade was going to depend on what happened *here* in the next five minutes. The Mercenary lurked in the far back corner of the room. She arched her eyebrows in his direction, then tapped a pen on a notepad. His stomach took a dive that had nothing to do with burned rice.

He sought refuge in Beth, who was watching him. She'd dressed for the part, though no one else ever did. Her grandmother's gauzy white gown practically screamed Juliet. Or imminent disaster.

Beth had been tardy for both of their classes together this morning, then spilled the contents of four loose-leaf notebooks in the hallway. When he'd asked if she was all right, she'd muttered something about Ni having left town early for spring break. Which seemed irrelevant. He suspected his partner had freaked.

We could not *do this. We could just accept a lower grade and perform the whole thing somewhere else.*

But they really couldn't. There wasn't time. They had used up every single possible day of rehearsal. And even if the Mercenary would have *allowed* them to undermine her schedule and move the scene, they couldn't because they had blocked out the whole thing to work here. It was do or die. Now.

Salva strode forward, dropped the tray on purpose, and gestured for his boys to drum-roll the table. They complied. Any excuse for a drum roll.

He vaulted over the corner of Numero Uno and skidded across the floor for his grand entrance, coming to a sharp halt at Beth's table.

Every sound in the cafeteria ceased.

She was dead. Her back arched across the table's surface, her knees crumpled sideways. Dramatic.

"'Here lies Juliet,'" he said, "'and her beauty makes this vault a feasting presence full of light. Death, lie thou there, by a dead man interr'd.'"

That got the crowd members. They knew now what the scene was going to be.

A rim of heads rose as people stood up at the edges of the room.

Salva fell to his knees on the floor. "'How oft when men are at the point of death have they been merry! Which their keepers call a lightning before death.'" He stood and stepped to the side of the table closest to Beth. "'O my love!'" Without intention, he brushed a stray strand of hair from her cheek.

She didn't move, or even flinch. She really was excellent at playing dead.

He was talking about her crimson lips now, and from the nearby table, Pepe was standing, shouting something suggestive.

Perfect.

Salva had thought about letting his best friend in on the whole plan, but decided against it. Technically, it was outside the rules to prep someone who wasn't in the scene. As with the drum roll, Pepe didn't need prepping to ham it up.

Salva made a skewering motion as though thrusting a sword at his best friend. "'Tybalt, liest thou there in thy bloody sheet?'" The move was a gamble. Though not much of one.

His best friend collapsed as though dead.

The audience erupted.

Salva stumbled back, grabbed at his own shirt, and reeled off his next line. "'O, what more favor can I do to thee, than with that hand that cut thy youth in twain to sunder his that was thine enemy?'" He splayed his hand in a beseeching manner toward his best friend. "'Forgive me, cousin!'"

"We'll see about that!" Pepe shouted back.

The audience roared.

Salva kept in character and waited out the applause. He knew he was good.

After all, Beth had trained him.

"'Ah, dear Juliet . . .'" He walked around her, because it would have been really boring just doing the whole speech looking at her, and the scene had needed more movement before getting to the poison.

During the bit with Pepe, students had started to joke and whisper, but the room drifted now to silence.

"'Why art though yet so fair?'" Salva scaled the table, and eased down, his knees straddling one of hers.

Whistles launched from the corners of the room.

"'Shall I believe that unsubstantial death is amorous . . .'" He cupped her chin in his hand, then traced the backs of his fingers along the side of her face. "'And that the lean abhorred monster keeps thee here in dark to be his paramour?'"

The whistles grew louder.

She was trembling.

Remember to breathe, he told himself. *Dios mío,* he was only half done. The next several lines rattled off his tongue. "'For fear of that, I still will stay with thee; and never from this palace of dim night depart again.'" He ran his fingers through her hair. *Thank God it was the last time he had to do that.*

"'. . . And shake the yoke of inauspicious stars from this world-wearied flesh.'" He lifted her chest and shook her torso. She fell forward against his shoulder. Her hair was everywhere: in his face, in his mouth. He had to spit it out surreptitiously as he dropped her back.

God, she was gorgeous. "'Eyes, look your last!'" He let himself peruse her entire figure. *The last time.*

More whistles, but he wasn't really hearing them. His heart was beating faster than it should, and he was in the middle of an adrenaline rush. "Arms, take your last embrace!" He pulled her once again to him, this time her chest against his. Her heart against his own, beating just as hard.

His hands moved to her shoulders, his eyes to her mouth. "'And, lips, O you the doors of breath . . .'" *He* was out of breath. Her mouth was partly open. Her eyes were closed, and Salva knew, right then, that he was never going to get another chance. "'. . . seal with a righteous kiss.'"

And his mouth was on hers. Not briefly. Not lightly. But long and deep, and *my God, she was kissing him back.* Maybe this was one of those dreams he'd been having ever since second rehearsal. But it didn't feel that way. It felt a hell of a lot better.

He came up for air and found the audience still there—saw the mouths forming screams and whistles that might have been a problem if he could have heard them over the desperate roaring in his own head.

Somehow he finished the monologue, drank from the poisoned goblet, and died.

By the inconstant moon! Beth's head screamed. He had kissed her. After all the rehearsals in which she had wished he would kiss her. In which he had pulled her close, then released her as though *she* was the poison. Beth opened her eyes to find him dead. *Thank the heavens.* She could never have finished the scene otherwise. She wasn't at all sure she could finish it now, but her mouth opened and words came out: "'What's here?'" Her eyes flew to the carton in his curled hand.

Why had he kissed her?

She reached for the goblet and had to pry it from his fingers. His hand was warm. Like his chest. He had been so close when he had pulled her to him—his heart beating so fast. At a whole other level for the performance.

Maybe that was what the kiss was about. Some kind of ploy to impress his friends.

"'O churl!'" She tossed the carton into the audience, then thrust his chin back with the heel of her hand. "'Drunk all, and left no friendly drop to help me after?'"

It was utterly unfair. That he could die and leave her to complete the performance.

She touched her fingers to his mouth. "'Thy lips are warm.'"

Good God, they had been. They had been strong and intense, and she would never in her entire life forget the feeling of that warmth on hers.

"'Noise?'" She whirled her head around as if searching the crowd, but it was all a blur. She hadn't made out a single face, other than his, since opening her eyes. "'Then I'll be brief. O happy dagger!'"

She snatched the foil-encased weapon clipped to the neckline of her bodice and pulled it out.

"'This is thy sheath.'" The tinfoil glittered with promise.

She plunged it to her belly, wrenching gasps from the crowd.

"'There rust . . .'" She curled over the weapon, then released her grip, allowing the foil to tumble to the floor.

"'And let me die.'"

Her back arched, and she fell—in a cross—over his chest, her head to the side, her arm dangling.

The applause was immediate. And loud. *Really loud.*

She made herself count ten, then lifted off his chest and scrambled from the table. He was right behind her. She didn't look at him—couldn't. Not yet. It was much better to soak in the realization that they had done exactly what they had hoped. The entire cafeteria was drum-rolling now. Nothing could take this rush away.

Salva's hand touched her elbow. She assumed he wanted her to bow so she gave a deep Juliet-like curtsy.

But he had not bowed.

His hand was back at her elbow, and it was tightening. He bent down to talk right into her ear, or she wouldn't have heard. "Markham."

She glanced up. And saw the principal glaring back at her. *Fie!*

"Sorry," Salva said.

13

LANGUAGE
BARRIER

Salva had never been in a Cell before. He had been in the Pen, for ASB meetings. He'd even been in Markham's office, acting as a witness when Pepe got himself in trouble, and, of course, for that lovely chat at the start of the year about AP English. But Salva had never previously been assigned to wait in one of the cheap particleboard stalls on either side of the secretary's desk.

The principal had called his father. At work.

God, this is not happening. But it was. Salva's insides had squeezed together when *Papá* had walked into the building. Markham, moving his large frame faster than memory could recall, had intercepted Señor Resendez right at the counter, then led him directly behind closed blinds into the principal's office. *Making certain I don't sway him toward my side of the story.*

Like that would have happened.

Plus, Salva didn't merit a side of the story. He shot a glance across the Pen at the Cell holding Beth. Her head was down on the desk. All he could see was the slumped back of that gauzy dress. She didn't deserve to be here, much less the half-day in-school suspension they had both been dealt. And the phone call. Which was worse. *Far* worse.

Salva had tried to explain—that the kiss had been all his idea—during his one-on-one interrogation with Markham.

But it hadn't gone over too well. "I sure as hell know the difference between a mutual display of affection and her giving you a slap in the face." The principal had glowered.

Now if Markham chose to swear in front of Salva's father, *that* might lose some points. But Salva knew exactly how the conversation in the closed office was really going. His father would agree with everything the principal said. Because Markham was the authority. His job was to help students have a good future. He deserved respect. *Yada, yada, yada.*

"Salvador." The principal's door opened. "Come in."

And Salva exchanged one cramped space for another, walking into the office with his head up. Okay, he'd done something stupid. He'd take the hit for it. But no way was he going to look cowed into submission. It'd been a kiss, for goodness' sake, not a line of cocaine.

"Salvador," said the principal, already seated as he gestured at a chair wedged between the front of his desk and the wall. Salva sat and locked his eyes on Markham. *Easier than facing Papá*—whose presence loomed to the right, in the only corner not occupied by a file cabinet. "Your father and I have discussed the incident in the cafeteria," Markham continued. "And I have been telling him the reason this most disturbs me is because, until today, you have been what I considered to be a leader in this school."

What *you* considered to be a leader?

"As the head of the ASB"—the principal locked his thick hands together and leaned forward, negating what little space there was—"you are expected not only to follow the rules, but to serve as a role model to the rest of the student body."

Yeah, yeah. Salva got it. He had embarrassed the school. Because he was the ASB president, and all those kids from the cafeteria were going to go home talking about what he and Beth had done for their project—which was what they had hoped would happen. But then some of those kids' parents were going to freak out, probably the same parents who thought their precious children were being corrupted by all the other teens at Liberty High, and Markham wanted to be able to tell those freaked-out parents that he'd dealt with the problem— that there were *no* exceptions to rules in the student handbook, even for the student body president.

"Yes, sir, I understand." Salva threw in the "sir" for good measure because he knew his father expected it.

"I'm not sure you do." Markham eased his pudgy fingers over the formal discipline slip he'd written up twenty minutes before. "To be clear, if anything like this ever happens again, you will risk losing your place as president."

The hell I will! For a kiss? Salva's gaze drilled into Markham's muddy brown eyes. This was the guy who had told Salva he had no choice but to take on Julie Tri-Ang's spot—that if someone else wanted to run for *vice* president, that was up to Nalani, but Liberty High had to have a leader from the very first week of the school year, and Salva was it. "I'm an elected officer."

"Then prove yourself worthy of your post."

Worthy! He'd done more than his share for this school. And Principal Markham's friggin' reputation. Salva was the reason Liberty High had won the county math contest four years in a row. He was the reason they'd had a science Odyssey team in the state final for the past two years. He was on the football team. He'd organized the service project that had given six tons of food to the food bank. He had run the fund-raiser that had raked in enough dough to put up a new school sign so the people driving by the building didn't think the place was just another prison getting forced on the county.

"Salvador." That was his father, waiting for a respectfully submissive remark.

"It will not happen again, Principal Markham." *Screw the "sir."* The guy could prove *himself* worthy of his post.

Señor Resendez stood up. "Principal Markham, I think that Salva should not be allowed to remain in school today. I will take him home with me now."

This was great. Just great! Even Markham knew the kiss didn't merit an out-of-school suspension, but *Papá* was going to yank Salva out of the building anyway.

The principal looked doubtful, like he thought Señor Resendez might try to sneak his son off for an early vacation.

As if. Salva knew exactly what waited for him at home. Crucifixion.

"Salva's mother," his father continued—*No. That was* not *fair*—"and I always believe our children should value school. Salva needs to come home and work so he understands what life has for him if he does not appreciate his education."

There was no way even Markham could misread that speech.

The principal stretched out his hand in a forthright gesture. "It was a pleasure, Mr. Resendez." They shook.

A frigging pleasure. Salva stepped outside the cramped office.

To his horror, his father blew past him to confront Beth. "Who are your parents?" he asked.

Her face turned pale as she sat erect, then brushed the wrinkles from her dress. "My mother is Rachel Courant. She works at the Eastside Hotel."

Señor Resendez grunted. "I see."

Salva seriously doubted his father saw a thing, other than the fact that he didn't have any connection with this girl's parents.

"*Hijo.*" Señor Resendez ordered his son to go.

But Salva didn't move. Because for the first time since the performance, Beth was looking at *him*. He wanted to explain— though he wasn't sure what to say. He knew he should apologize again, no question. But what he wanted even more, what he really wanted, was to know how she had felt about that kiss.

Had she hated it?

Was she furious with him?

Had she died of embarrassment in front of the entire student body?

Because it hadn't felt like she had. It had felt like maybe she had wanted that kiss as much as he had. Like she might not mind if he did it again.

Señor Resendez's hand tightened on Salva's shoulder, breaking into his son's thoughts, and escorted him out.

The only sounds on the pickup ride home were the rattle of the dash, the jerking of the gearshift, and the coughing of the engine. Salva knew better than to talk first. He had never before been on the receiving end of his father's silent treatment. But he had seen the silence explode—the year Miguel had been kicked out.

The vehicle choked and died about twenty feet from the single wide, then coasted the remaining distance.

Señor Resendez failed to exit. Leaving his youngest son trapped against the nonfunctioning door.

"You work with this girl on a project for English class?" his father finally said.

"*Sí, Papá.*"

"You do not have a relationship with this girl?"

"No." Salva didn't, at least not in the way his father meant.

Señor Resendez climbed out of the pickup, allowing his son to follow.

Lucia's half-ass car was already parked by the gate. *Not good.* She wasn't supposed to show up at home until after five o'clock.

But she was reading on the couch in the Shrine. Or pretending to read, a massively thick textbook titled *Psychological Theory.* "*¡Papá!*" she said, acting surprised. "*¿Qué pasó?*" Salva noted she didn't mark her place when she set the book down.

Señor Resendez launched into the Lecture. "I am *home,*" he said, "since I receive a phone call *que se requiere* I leave my place at work without warning. Because my *son* is a disgrace to the school."

Lucia's eyes went wide, though for once she kept her mouth shut.

Papá strode up to the perennial altar above the fake fireplace.

Salva looked away. From the candles that smelled like his mother, the dried flowers he knew sat beside them, and the photo that threatened to tear him apart.

His father continued, "But the answer to your question, Lucia, is that I am *here* because your mother no want you to grow up ignorant, serving berries to the *gringos* and *turistas* in Michoacán. Because when she becomes pregnant with Casandra she says she will not raise any more children in *la pobreza.*"

"And then," he added, "when I want to go north without her, she say I can get a visa for her also, or I can get a divorce. So I work for all the wrong people to get the bribe so my whole *familia* can come into *los Estados Unidos.* Then your mother, she works pregnant, so the farmer won't accuse her of lying and send us back."

Salva had heard the whole spiel a thousand times. How education, education, education was the answer. How all the Resendez children were going to have a better future because they had the chance to go to school here in the United States.

"Your mother and I, we work very hard," *Papá* continued, "all so you, Lucia"—here the speech departed from form—"can waste your time and money by flunking all your classes."

"*Papá*, I'm not—"

"And my son." *The vaunted son line.* "Who has all the brains and every opportunity to make something of himself can throw it away. On *nada!*"

Salva's head throbbed like the inside of a *guitarrón*.

"You both"—Señor Resendez pounded the mantel—"go to pass the afternoon outside. Turn the earth and plant the garden. And think what your life would be like planting onions for *los gringos*. Or back in *México* for *los ricos*."

Salva flinched.

Lucia was propelling her brother toward the back of the house. "*¡Sí, Papá!*" she shouted, pausing long enough in the kitchen to grab two sets of work gloves from a cabinet. She slapped Salva's against his stomach, then dragged him out the door.

"*Brillante*," she said. "What did you do?"

He didn't answer, just went to the tools propped in the corner of the patio, grabbed a shovel, and headed for the far left corner of the property. The entire backyard was the garden.

Lucia followed him. "*Por favor*, Salva, tell me. I'll find out anyway. I have friends at your school, you know."

He jammed the shovel into the earth.

"*Mira*," she said, "it's not the end of the world."

He stepped on the flat upper edge, driving the blade deeper. Four years. Four years of solid A's and one B. Seven months of study sessions. All so he could become yet another of his father's disappointments.

Beth struggled to find her courage as she stared, from behind the gate, at the entrance to the Resendez residence. The door was green. Faded. With no relation to the color scheme of the porch or the rest of the single wide, as though someone had painted the entrance with grander plans and then forgotten to finish the job, or run out of money.

She had never knocked on this door before, a failure that made the decision to do so now—three hours after she and Salva had both been sent to the principal's office—much worse. Why had she never suggested they go to Salva's house to study? Or taken him his homework on a day when he was sick?

Because he's never sick.

That was, he had never missed school, even when he was sick.

She would have noticed.

Stop it, Beth Courant; you're stalling.

She gathered the folds of her grandmother's gown to avoid

ripping it on the gate, then lifted the latch and headed up the short path. *There is nothing wrong with telling him he got an A on his project.* Except that she wasn't really here to talk about the project. Well, she was. In a way. She couldn't just leave things as they were, without asking. Or trying to ask. What that kiss had meant.

Though going over to his place could be viewed as desperate. *He made the first move. It certainly wasn't me.*

But she was making one now.

She had run out of space on the path. The porch was clean. Immaculate. No weeds grew up through the cracks in the wood. And the hand-carved BIENVENIDOS sign hung perfectly horizontal. Chimes with silver moons and suns dangled above her. *The doorbell, Beth. Push the bell, and maybe he'll answer it.*

The green door swung inward. Not Salva.

His father, the large confrontational man who had asked about her parents, as if he thought she was plotting against the school and misleading the principal about whom to call. Which wasn't the case. She knew her mother was just too busy to answer the phone.

Backbone, Beth. "H-hello, sir. Is Salva here?"

The only response was a frown.

"I'm Beth." She felt compelled to reintroduce herself even though it was obvious by the frown that he had not forgotten who she was. She stretched out a hand, then pulled it back when he failed to acknowledge it. "I-I've been helping Salva in

AP English. Well, actually we've been helping each other. It's a challenging class."

"My son is not here," he said.

"Oh." Until this moment, she had not been 100 percent certain of whether she *wanted* Salva to be home. Suddenly, she realized how much she *had* wanted it. And how important it was that his father *not* hate her.

"I know we made a mistake today." She twisted the chiffon strands dangling from the belt at her waist. "And we're both sorry for that."

"Are you?" Mr. Resendez raised his eyebrows, his dark forehead folding together in wide furrows.

"Yes, sir. But . . ." After serving her suspension in the office, she had gone to see the Mercenary. "I wanted to let Salva know that it wasn't all bad. I mean, all the work we put in wasn't wasted."

The man glanced over his shoulder, as if he might walk away.

Beth rushed to explain. "We earned an A on our project."

The muscles in his face didn't relax.

Her left arm began to sting. "Could you tell him that, please?"

His gaze went to her elbow.

She realized she'd wrapped it in the chiffon and begun to cut off the circulation.

"You earned an A on your project." He repeated her words.

"Yes," Beth said, hurrying to unwind the fabric. "Our Shakespeare project. It was very important—worth a third of our grade."

"I understand your message," he said.

And the green door swung shut in her face.

"What is this message about from the school?" Ms. Courant's worn voice grated through the darkness from the threshold of Beth's bedroom later that evening.

Beth rolled away from the question, burying herself behind her eyelids and regretting her failure to climb under the bedcovers. She'd heard the tires on gravel, the fight with the screen door, and the footsteps. But she hadn't had the forethought to plan ahead. Her eyes burned from exhausted tears, and her head throbbed. She didn't have the strength to deal with this tonight.

The light flipped on, followed by a sigh. Something scraped across the floor, then papers crackled and something else shuffled.

Why can't she respect the barrier? There was no safety in this place anymore. Ever.

"Tell me about the phone call," the invader said.

"It's nothing." Beth silently cursed the raw croak in her voice.

"If it was nothing, you wouldn't be pretending to sleep in that dress."

Because I wouldn't have to pretend. You wouldn't bother coming to talk to me.

Beth rolled up into a seated, huddled position, her head down, her arms hugging the wrinkled skirt of her grandmother's dress to her knees. It was probably ruined now. Like everything. Beth felt trapped in the maelstrom of the events of the day, ending with that green door shut in her face. "It's just Principal Markham making a big thing out of nothing."

The bed mattress tilted as her mother sank down at her daughter's side. "Well, just what is this . . . nothing? You know I can't take off work, but I *am* going to return that call; and if I have to hear it from him first—"

"We did our Shakespeare project today."

"What?"

You don't know. Because you don't care what's happening in my life. "Beth."

My name used as a weapon. "It was a performance for AP English. My partner and I did the death scene from *Romeo and Juliet.*"

"'O happy dagger.'"

The quote shook her. She had forgotten her mother had been an English major before dropping out.

"That's quite a scene," added Ms. Courant.

An incredible scene. And now it was ruined forever.

Beth had allowed herself to hope, she realized. Fear, anxiety, hesitation: they had all been present as she had climbed those porch steps to Salva's home. But the most dangerous emotion had been *hope,* crushed now by his father's anger.

She pressed her fingers to her temples, wanting to talk with someone other than her mother. But there was no one. After facing Mr. Resendez's disapproval, Salva would probably never speak to Beth again. And Ni had gone on vacation yesterday and *still* didn't know about him. Unlike the entire rest of the school.

"We earned an A," Beth croaked. As if that mattered. As if it mattered to anyone.

"Impressive."

Was that sarcasm? Or just a prompt to dig out an explanation?

Beth tried to steel herself for the task. And failed. Her hands were cold, and goose bumps ran the length of her arms. Her mother had no tolerance for boys. Boys were a problem who got you pregnant, then abandoned you so you had to drop out of school, live in a trailer, and raise a child you didn't want.

Just get it over with. Maybe if she yells it will numb the rest of the pain. The words burst forward in a suicidal rush. "Well, there was this kiss in the death scene, and Principal Markham got all disturbed by it because there aren't supposed to be any public displays of affection at school." Beth stared very hard at a whirlpool print on her bedspread.

Her mother's response was expressionless. "You were acting?"

"Yes."

"The death scene from *Romeo and Juliet*?"

"Yes."

"And the principal was upset by a kiss in the performance?"

"Yes."

"Oh . . ." Her mother let out a long, relentless breath. "Is that all?" She stood, without waiting for the answer, and withdrew, muttering something about the small-time thinking in this town. Leaving her daughter once again.

Alone.

14

MELTED ICE CREAM

"Mira, Salva." His father aimed the metal spatula away from the backyard grill toward a plate on the red plastic-covered picnic table. *"Tome este plato a Charla."*

Salva eyed the plate heaped with barbecued chicken in poblano salsa, fried greens, jalapeño cornbread, gazpacho salad, and pineapple flan. Char would never eat that much in her life. *"Papá."* He tried to tell his father she would probably rather select her own food.

"¡Llévelo a ella!" the older man insisted, giving Salva a push across the Resendez patio toward the folding lounge chair, where Char had stretched her long bare legs out in the sun.

Señora Mendoza vacated her own seat, beside her daughter, and took another place on the opposite side of Lucia.

Salva groaned. When were *los adultos* going to accept that he and Char were *not* getting together?

The impromptu barbecue between the two families had

been *Papá's* idea, a sudden inspiration as Señor Resendez and Char's mother had been yakking on the steps after church. It *was* an extraordinarily warm day for the first weekend of spring break. Talia, Casandra, and Char's younger brother, Renaldo, were dripping Popsicles all over the cement.

Señora Mendoza glanced at her sticky son, then shook her head, smiling. *"¡Vaya al agua!"* She waved at the younger kids to go cool off in the front-yard sprinkler.

Salva envied their escape as he tried to deliver the plate.

Char arched her shaped eyebrows and shook her head at the food. "I'm not eating," she said.

He turned around.

"What?" Señor Resendez had abandoned his post at the grill. He put a hand on Salva's shoulder and rotated his son back toward Char. "How can you come to a barbecue and not eat? You have to eat."

"I'm going over to Linette's house for dinner at four," she replied.

"Is only one o'clock now," said *Papá.* "Lots of time to be hungry again." He waved his spatula as if that was the end of the topic, then turned to make a comment in Spanish to her mother.

Salva set the plate down at Char's feet. She'd be better off if she just picked at the food. It would save her the exhausting experience of arguing with his father. "Would you like a drink?" Salva asked.

"A gentleman, your son," Señora Mendoza said in careful English. "I wish more boys in this town were like him. *Sí*, Charla?"

Which would have been a great time for Char to mention Pepe, though he didn't exactly come off as the gentleman type. Still, if things were moving as fast as he *claimed*, it was about time Char had the guts to acknowledge her relationship with Salva's best friend.

"I'll have a Diet Coke," she said.

The cooler had only Diet Pepsi, but Salva didn't stick around to clarify details.

Unfortunately, the drinks weren't far enough away to avoid the conversation. "Where you go to college, Charla?" Señor Resendez glanced at Señora Mendoza, who nodded back.

Char didn't answer.

"You have to make a decision soon, no?" he kept after her. "I ask my son, and he say he waits to hear back from more colleges. But you have to know kind of already."

Char shot a glance across the striped back of her chair at Salva.

Like he was going to rescue her? No way. At least not as long as she kept holding out about his best friend. Salva picked up a Pepsi for himself, then plunged his hand into the ice for Char's drink.

She finally answered, "I guess maybe I'll take some classes at the job center."

Both her mother and Señor Resendez frowned. "That's not

going to college," *Papá* replied. "That's just basic skills. You don't want a basic job."

Salva cringed.

Just because Char didn't have a father didn't mean that *Papá* had to act the part. *Papá* had never really understood how hard school was for her. And there was the whole illegal thing. How did he think she was going to get around that?

"You apply for Lucia's school?" Señor Resendez continued. "You could be her roommate."

"*¡Papá!*" Lucia said. "I'm going to graduate this year!"

"We'll see." His tone was not convinced.

She abandoned her emptied plate and marched off in a huff, across the very well-turned garden.

Señor Resendez kept talking to Char. "Maybe Salva could help you fill out the applications."

Oh God. No more. No more driving lessons or extra tutoring or delivering plates.

Salva dropped off the Diet Pepsi at Char's side, then followed Lucia.

She was leaning, her spine against the high scalloped boards of the backyard fence. "He doesn't get it," she said, banging her knuckles on the wooden surface. "Like Friday. No one in college waits until five P.M. on Friday to begin their vacation. They just take their last class and go."

"At least he's not trying to hook you up." Salva leaned his back against the nearby gate.

Lucia's grimace turned into a smirk. "So . . . this girl who played Juliet . . ."

Well, that hadn't taken long. He wondered which of her friends had gabbed on him. Salva shook up his pop can and cracked the lid, letting the liquid shoot in his sister's direction.

Lucia dodged the spray. "She's the one who was helping you study this winter, right?"

Was his sister's mind hardwired to this stuff? He took a drink and rotated, leaning his arms over the chest-high gate.

"What's her name?" she asked.

"Beth." Salva exhaled as if he'd been holding his breath since Friday.

"Mmm-hmm. Is she pretty?"

He shrugged. "She's okay." From an unbiased viewpoint that was honest, wasn't it? He hadn't realized she was beautiful until he'd gotten to know her. Well, he'd known her a long time, but he hadn't really—

"Uh-huh. So you aren't dating yet. You know you should probably tell *Papá* you're interested. Give him a little time to get used to the idea."

Right. The only thing his father would hear was the fact that she wasn't *mexicana.* "Beth doesn't deserve to be treated like she's second-class," Salva found himself saying. "She's a much nicer girl than the *chica Papá* thinks I ought to be going out with."

Lucia shot a glance toward the patio. "Yeah, well, that's because he doesn't know what *la chica* is up to. But I didn't ask about Char." She poached the Pepsi. "I asked about Beth."

"All right, she's pretty," he admitted.

"And smart?"

"And smart."

"Good," Lucia said. "It's about time you found somebody who was."

Was it? He changed the subject. "I've had enough *familia* this weekend, you know." He pricked himself on the wire holding the gate.

She laughed. "You were working at the plant yesterday."

"Yeah, with *Papá*. And he got me signed up for all of spring break." Salva knew the hours weren't part of his punishment, but it felt like they were. "Nice of him, isn't it?"

Lucia took a drink from the pop can, then flipped it over and shook out the final drops. "I don't know, Salva. I don't know whether it's better to be you, with too much *familia*, or me, with not enough."

He started fiddling with the twisted wire. "You really think you're gonna finish school this year?" The answer was more important than he wanted to admit.

"Yes. I might need to retake a course during the summer, but then I'm coming home. And help take care of Talia and Casandra."

"You really want that?"

"*Sí*," she said, and set the pop can down on one of the fence posts.

He knew his desire to believe her was selfish—that he wanted her to stay. To alleviate the guilt he was going to feel at leaving his younger sisters. But Salva also wanted to believe—somehow—that he wasn't robbing Lucia of her future in order to live his own. "You could apply to go to nursing school," he said, "instead of just working at the retirement home."

She wrinkled her nose. "With my grades? You go be the doctor in the family."

No. He'd seen enough of doctors when he was thirteen—doctors who couldn't offer his mother anything but bills. And guilt, about the fact that she hadn't come to the hospital earlier.

Salva blocked the memory, pricking himself again on the wire. At least *Papá* hadn't been hammering away on the topic of what his son was going to do with his life. Though Salva was sure if he returned to the patio, the subject was waiting for him. But he wasn't going back for that. If he slipped through the gate, he could be out of hearing distance before his father even realized he was short one child to pressure.

Salva unwound the wire.

Lucia was eyeing him. "Do you really think it's a good idea to push *Papá*?"

"He's busy chatting up Señora Mendoza. I don't know why *he* doesn't just marry *her*."

His sister blinked. "Because he's still in love with our mother."

Salva shoved open the gate. The dirt road behind the house was overgrown with weeds—the next job on his list of chores, no doubt. But this was Sunday. He'd sowed the frigging garden and then had to work at the plant yesterday. Plus, he had to work all this week. Today was *his* afternoon. And he was taking it.

He launched into a jog, down the dirt alley, and within moments was sprinting on pavement. He didn't care where he was headed, just away. Maybe Tosa's. Maybe Pepe's. He and his best friend did need to talk.

Salva slowed his pace as he neared Main Street. His shoes were falling apart. He'd spent his fall shoe money on extracurricular fees, and now the rubber on the back of his left Nike was peeling away. Meanwhile, he had all of five dollars in his pocket. Everything else this month had gone into *El Banco de la Familia*.

Which was fine. He only had nine weeks left of high school anyway. Then nobody would be looking at his shoes.

Nine weeks. Was that possible? Two months with Pepe and Tosa and Char. Man, it seemed like he'd known them forever. Only two more months with—

Beth. She was standing across the street alone at the drive-in window. Barefoot, her sandals in her left hand.

For the first time all day, he appreciated the sun.

Salva scanned the area. It looked like she was really alone.

He crossed the road in his lousy shoes and walked up behind her. She was staring at the list of hard ice cream flavors. "Hey," he said, *hey* being the internationally recognized greeting for someone whose reputation you have just massacred along with your own. To his knowledge, Beth had never even been called into the principal's office before yesterday, much less spent an afternoon in a Cell.

She jumped about a foot in the air. Good thing she hadn't ordered yet.

"I suggest the chocolate," he said, "though Rocky Road is pretty good if you like nuts."

She gave him a defensive glare.

This was going to call for more than an apology.

The window opened with a grunt from the owner, who was balding, had a potbelly, and looked about fifty years old. *If I'm running a place like this when I'm fifty, please shoot me.*

Beth said, "A single scoop of bubblegum on a sugar cone, please."

That made Salva grin. Most teenage girls thought they were too mature for bubblegum. "I'll have chocolate," he said, "on a plain cone."

She squinted at him in the sunlight. "I was here first."

"I'm buying."

"I-I have the money," she stammered.

He guessed she didn't have enough experience sponging off guys. Char would have tried to make something out of the offer. Beth just stared at him like a deer in headlights, though a very pretty deer.

Two cones appeared in the window. She took hers, then

reached forward to pay. Salva intercepted, snagging her wrist. He dug his five dollars out of his pocket, paid, and collected the change. Then he picked up two napkins, wrapped one around his own cone, and offered her the extra. "Walk with me," he said, "down to the river."

She disdained the napkin.

"We should talk," he added. "Don't you think?"

Her eyes zipped around as if searching for a hidden audience, then slowed and finally settled on him. "I suppose." She bit into her brilliant blue ice cream speckled with pinks and greens.

He walked beside her. Close. About as close as he thought he could get away with. It was four blocks down to the river, the best four blocks of town. The trees were actually planted to provide shade along the sidewalks here, and the sidewalks were flat and kept up by the city, no cement tilting at a thirty-five-degree angle.

She didn't look like she was enjoying the atmosphere. Her shoulders were stiff, and despite the sandals in her hand, she kept plucking at her shorts as if trying to make them longer. He'd messed things up back at school, between the two of them. He ought to put it right. Come out with it, in the open. He swallowed the last bite of his cone. "Look, about what happened on Friday, I didn't mean . . . That is, I'm—"

"Don't." She picked up her pace. Her cone was vibrating.

Was she so angry she wouldn't let him apologize?

He had to lengthen his strides to keep up with her. "I just wanted to—"

"You're going to say you're sorry."

"I never meant—"

"I know you never meant it. Just don't say any more." She sped up again. He tried to grasp what was happening. Something didn't make any sense. She was running away, and his instincts told him that if he let her go—if he let her brush off the apology and refuse to talk about what had happened, then *everything* would be ruined.

He ditched his napkin in a painted garbage can and ran after her. "Wait." He took her elbow. "What is it you think I never meant?"

She was standing at the edge of the park, a great wide expanse of sloping grass and scattered trees. Neglected ice cream dripped down her fingers. "You don't have to worry," she said, her voice so soft he could barely hear. "I know you didn't mean for me to make anything out of the kiss."

The kiss? She thought he was trying to back out of his decision to kiss her? And the strange thing was, the idea had never occurred to him. It wasn't the kind of action he could back out of, kissing someone in front of the entire student body. He stepped closer. "I meant to apologize," he said gently, "for getting you into trouble. I wasn't going to apologize for the kiss."

"You weren't?" Her head came up, and those doe eyes looked straight into him.

"I didn't plan it." He shrugged. "It just kind of . . . happened."

She nodded as if this made any kind of sense, but then she turned away and headed across the park.

He tried to plan as he stripped off his shoes and socks, then sank his feet into the cool grass; but the attempt at strategy was impossible. She had no respect for anything less than solid truth. When he caught up with her, the remnants of her cone were gone. "Was your mother very angry?" he asked. They ought to get that out of the way—clear up exactly how much groveling he should be doing.

"No." Beth weaved around a giant maple. "She understood it was just a scene in a play."

What was that supposed to mean? That it was just acting? It hadn't just been acting on his part. The rest of it, yeah, but the kiss—well, he thought maybe he'd finally stopped acting. He'd been acting around Beth for months now, and he supposed he'd reached the point where it needed to stop.

He let that realization sink into his brain as the river came into view, not a wide crystal blue of perfection, but a gray-green curve with a mossy tinge. From the edge, an empty crescent of sand rose up, followed by weeds, then sharp rocks guarding the upper rim.

"Y-your father, though," Beth said, continuing across the grass. "I-I guess he hasn't forgiven you yet. I thought maybe he would when I told him about the Shakespeare grade, but—"

"When you what?" Salva froze. He had been there, in the

Pen, for the entire four-second conversation between his father and Beth, and she hadn't said anything about a grade.

She turned back to look at him. "When I told him that we got an A on our Shakespeare project. Didn't he tell you?"

She'd seen his father again? When, *when* had this happened, and what had his father said to her? Had *Papá* gone looking for her? Or called her home to tell her mother what Beth had done wrong? "When did you talk alone with my father?" Salva crossed the gap between them.

"Fri-Friday." She backed away. "I-I went to your place after school. He didn't tell you?"

No, his father hadn't told him. This was out of line. It was one thing to punish Salva for his own stupid behavior. But it was absolutely *not* okay that Beth had come over and his father had failed to mention it. "What did he say?"

"He just . . ." A wince of pain crossed her face, and she turned, ducking under the branches of a tree—a giant wide parasol of a tree with white flowers that had just begun to drip petals onto the green beneath them. "He didn't really say anything."

She was keeping something back. What had *happened* to her?

"Beth—" Salva followed her under the branches.

"Your father said you weren't there, and I-I left."

But I was there, in the backyard, working on the garden. Suddenly *Papá* was not the same person Salva had known all his life. If not letting him talk to her was part of his punishment, that was one thing. But making her feel bad? Lying to her? Not even saying she had come. His hand gripped the tree trunk. "I can't believe . . ."

The expression on Beth's face changed. Her fingers touched his arm gently, wrenching him out of his anger. "But we did get an A, Salva. And it was the highest mark in the class. The Mercenary told me."

"You're not afraid of anything, are you?" he said.

The fingers fled. "Why would you say that?"

"You came to my home the day we were suspended. That takes guts. And then you talked to my father after how rude he was to you in the Pen. He's not usually like that, Beth. I don't know what's wrong with him." Except Salva was afraid that maybe his father was more prejudiced than Salva had ever realized. *Papá* had been through a lot, put up with a lot from a lot of privileged people in his life.

But that didn't excuse being unfair to Beth.

Salva sat down under the tree. If he sat, this talk would last longer, and he was in no hurry for it to end. No hurry for her to go anywhere. He reached for her hand and tugged her down beside him.

She started gathering the white blossoms within her reach.

And he found himself telling her his own take on fear. "I always defend against getting hurt, you know. Never put myself in a situation that I think might be uncomfortable."

"Everyone likes you." She scooped the blossoms into a pile, then continued to gather.

"I don't know. I'm so careful not to upset people; I think maybe not everyone knows who I am."

"Are you telling me Pepe and Tosa don't know who you are?"

"Oh, not them," he said, then paused. "Though, well, being careful about what I say—it might be more true with my friends than with anyone else. Sometimes it's easier to tell strangers what you're thinking than your friends."

Her hands paused in their gathering. "And I'm more like a stranger."

Boy, had he blown that one. Hadn't even seen that coming. *Brilliant, Salva.*

"No," he told her directly. "You're different. Like the one person I feel I can tell what I really think. And even if you hate it, you won't mock or take it the wrong way. You'll just tell me you hate it and then tell me why."

She hadn't told him she'd hated the kiss. In fact, she had been adamant that he *not* apologize for it.

"You're wrong about me," she said, looking up and meeting his gaze.

He didn't think he was wrong. He thought maybe he was finally getting things right.

"I am afraid," she continued. "I was afraid the first day you asked me to read your paper last fall, the one about Milton. And I've been afraid ever since."

Was she saying she was afraid of him? His every nerve rejected the idea.

"Do you know why I told you no that first day?" she asked. "Why I didn't want to help you?"

"Because I am a complete jerk and you knew sooner or later I'd land you in the principal's office?"

"I was afraid of you."

She *couldn't* be afraid of him.

Her hands dug into the grass. "Afraid I would fall in love with you and never mean anything more to you than a stupid mark on a stupid essay."

His heart pounded beneath his lungs. And he couldn't move.

The grass shredded. "I was afraid you would walk off," she added, "and never see me again, and I would never be able to forget you."

He didn't want her to forget him.

"So we're both afraid," she continued, those brown eyes very close. "We both hedge our bets, you with your friends and me with you."

Her chin was trembling.

His hand came up and touched it. Her chin. Her cheek. Her ear. Her neck. He pulled her head to him. And his lips met hers. Soft.

So soft, at first, like melted ice cream. And then deeper.

And her lips were answering his. Her touch was answering his. And she was coming with him. He fell onto his back in the grass. His hands were in her hair, down her neck, her shoulders, in her hair again.

Her hands were on his shoulders, in the grass, then his hair. Her chest was over his. She was propped above him on her elbows.

Then she wasn't. Her tongue was meeting his and her heart was beating the same wild, rapid rhythm right above his own.

A stranger's voice ripped apart the moment. "Ugh! You kids today. Can't even leave each other alone in public." An old woman, her hand attached to the leash of a little yapping dog, shuffled across Salva's line of vision.

Vision still obscured by the falling veil of Beth's hair.

Beth looked at him. They both looked in the direction of the departing duo.

Then looked at each other again. Beth's eyes were shining. A brilliant warm brown. It was ridiculous really. Seven months he'd been meeting with her in private, and the first two times they'd kissed, they'd been scolded for kissing in public.

She collapsed on top of him, and they both laughed.

15

FRIEND OR FOE

Slam! Clang! Someone was battling with the screen door. Beth rolled over under the bedcovers. She didn't want to fight. She wanted to return to the dream in which the colors had all been muted, save the deep orange-gold glow of the sun dropping over the horizon of manufactured homes and vacant lots. And *he* had been walking her home.

"Beth!" A familiar voice shattered the sunset. "School!" Nalani was shaking her.

Cripes! It was Monday—the Monday after break.

"You didn't set your alarm," Ni accused.

Beth rolled out of bed, literally. She was trapped in the tangle of bedcovers.

"Where is it?" Ni asked, now digging through the bureau. Items began to fly in her friend's direction: a bra, a pair of socks, underwear.

"I-I don't know," said Beth. She managed to untangle herself from everything except the sheet, which was coiled around her waist.

"Got it." Ni plucked a blue alarm clock from the top drawer, then started pushing buttons.

The sheet finally fell away. Beth tugged off her nightshirt and began scrambling into her underclothes.

"Jeans?" Ni was now staring into an open drawer.

"Um . . . laundry basket."

A pair of semi-clean jeans hit Beth in the chest, followed by a turquoise blouse she hadn't seen since last year's academic awards ceremony. Her friend must have braved the closet.

"Get dressed. I'll get breakfast," said Nalani, dashing from the room.

Beth complied, detoured to the bathroom, doused her face with water from the sink, swished her mouth with toothpaste, and emerged to begin the daunting search for her backpack. *Thank goodness for best friends!* Ni had been picking her up—and rescuing her on the way to school—since they were twelve.

"It's by the couch," Nalani shouted from the kitchen counter.

Sure enough, the bane of Beth's existence lay in front of the sofa. Along with her shoes.

"Go ahead and tie them," Ni said.

Beth tied the laces, then glanced at the kitchen clock. The hour hand was aimed at the three. The power must have blinked at some point in the last nine days.

"We've got ten minutes," her best friend said, handing over

a raspberry jam sandwich. "Let's go." The screen door was propped open, no doubt as a time-saver.

Beth slammed both doors on her way out.

The sky was gray, and puddles of the same shade lined the street's edge. "So . . ." Her best friend untwisted the pink strap of her book bag, then swerved around the puddles to higher pavement. "How was your break?" She launched into rapid strides.

Beth struggled to keep the pace. How was she to explain *everything* at a near sprint? About the kiss. And the second kiss. And how she hadn't heard anything from Salva since. Why hadn't Ni called while on her trip? She knew Ms. Courant wouldn't let her daughter use the cell phone or long distance.

Though to be fair, Beth hadn't exactly tried. *How am I going to explain what's going on with Salva when I don't really know myself?* "Um . . . how was Colorado?" Beth stalled. *An unwise choice.*

"Great," Ni said, and started reeling off places she'd been, things she'd seen, the names of twenty-five cousins she'd met—

This is stupid. You need to tell her, and you need to tell her now.

Everything Beth hadn't said over the past seven months swam in her head, along with guilt, chaos, and confusion.

The afternoon in the park with Salva had been incredible. For both of them. That kiss hadn't been platonic. Or tentative. Or at all questionable. At least it hadn't felt that way.

But then he hadn't called.

Maybe he couldn't while his father was so upset.

Or was she just searching for excuses?

The high school emerged in the distance—a dull gray prism. Beth felt her stomach tighten. Salva would be there, on the social podium that was his place at Liberty High.

"But we can talk about all that later," Ni was saying. "I know I've been a little distracted this winter."

Distracted? Beth's head was beginning to ache, and panic was climbing from the lining of her stomach to infect the rest of her body. *How am I going to endure this?* The mocking catcalls that were sure to arise from the students who could manage to remember ten days into the past, the disdain Salva would have to show for her in order to maintain his standing among his friends, the rejection she would have to endure . . .

Ni was still talking. "I thought maybe you had wanted to tell me something and that I was too—"

Beth was trying to listen, but terror had muffled her ears. The parking lot stretched before her now, an enormous pond of sunken asphalt.

"So are you going to tell me or not?" Ni suddenly blocked her path.

"What?" Beth had lost track of the conversation.

"Fine!" Ni snapped. *"Don't* tell me. *Don't* explain how you and Salva Resendez—whom you've had a crush on *forever*—wound up kissing in front of the entire school!" She whirled and marched across the parking lot.

Ouch. Beth knew she should chase after her best friend. But it was too difficult to move. To breathe. Because he was there on the front steps.

And at his side was Char Mendoza. And Pepe Real, Ricardo Tosa, Linette Kasing. They merged in a tight pack, energy passing from one to the next in the form of high fives, slaps on the back, and arms wrapped around the girls' waists. *You knew these were his friends. That they meant the world to him. That you could never mean as much to him as they do. You knew. You knew. You knew.*

The first bell rang, and the elite crowd rose up the stairs to claim their domain, the ominous gray building before Beth.

Who still couldn't move. She *had* known. But she had shunned the knowledge, cramming it into the narrow pragmatic part of her brain and refusing to let the truth ride through her blood to her chest. Until now.

This was going to be hell.

She sneaked in late for cit/gov, which meant the only desk available was clear across the room from Salva. They were watching a film, so it was not too hard to hurry out at the end without feeling ignored. In English there were some whistles and sexual comments about the scene from *Romeo and Juliet*, but between the Mercenary's glare and Salva's cool, the ribbing quickly died. He even backed up a comment Beth made during class discussion. But then AP English was their world—a world apart from all the friends he had told her he was afraid of upsetting.

The cafeteria, though, was ground zero. She hovered outside the lunchroom door, the noise and shouts from the interior blasting her in the face. Inside belonged to Pepe and Tosa and the girls who had made Beth's entire middle-school experience a misery. Because who could compete with Linette, of the blond hair and the snappy comebacks? And Char Mendoza, who made Beth feel like a crushed swallowtail under a spiked high heel?

Salva had always been with Char, long before the two of them had dated. He had walked her to school, picked her up, escorted her to events. No matter how long Beth had known him, Char had known him longer. And she would be sitting at his table.

I'm prepared, Beth told herself. *Prepared to walk right by that table without his even acknowledging my existence.*

And then it would be done.

The line would be drawn. And she would know exactly where she belonged in his world—somewhere outside it.

A dark ponytail brushed past her. A high head. Nalani. The need to repair things finally towed Beth across the threshold. "Listen, Ni." She followed her friend up to the main counter. "I'm sorry. I'm *extremely* sorry."

No response.

They each obtained a tray. "It's just," Beth added, "he asked me to help him, and I—you know I'm not very good at turning people down when they need my help."

Both girls picked out a spoon and fork.

"I wanted to tell you," Beth continued, "but I knew you

would say I was being stupid, and I knew I was being stupid, but . . ."

The height of Nalani's shoulders lowered, which meant Ni was listening. Though the noise in the cafeteria seemed to have increased, if that was possible. At least no one other than Nalani was paying heed to this confession, proof that no matter what had happened last week, Beth was just as invisible as she had always—

Warmth draped across her shoulders.

And the room went silent. Absolutely. Totally. Silent.

"Don't worry," Salva said softly, grinning down at her. "Markham can't flip out. He's stuck in the library with a parent. I just came from there."

Her voice didn't work.

Or her mind. Salva couldn't be there with his arm around her shoulders, announcing to the entire room in this one gesture that he was *with* her. Could he? The arm remained around her while their trays collected food. Then his hand ran smooth and flat across her back as he lowered his mouth to her ear. "So you ready for this?" he asked.

The silence in the cafeteria turned to whispers.

"R-ready for what?" she asked. *Dear God, is this really happening? Did I just become Salva Resendez's girlfriend?*

"Sitting with my friends."

Oh my God. She had. Her eyes flew to Ni, who looked just as stunned as everyone else in the cafeteria.

"I know you'd rather sit with Nalani," he said, "but we can

do that tomorrow. There's no avoiding Pepe. If I ignore him, he'll make my life a living hell. So we're going to have to do this today. All right?"

Was he truly asking? Because if he was, Beth had a sudden desire to beg for a reprieve. Then she saw Salva's chest rise in a halting stagger, and she realized he hadn't been asking if she would do this, but if she would do this *for him*. He was afraid.

She glanced at her best friend.

Ni responded at last, mouthing the word *Go!*

Beth went, the hand on her back steering her toward the most exclusive spot at Liberty High. The table was only half full. With Pepe beside Char. And Tosa with Linette.

Of course Salva was afraid, Beth thought. Ultimately, he was the one with something to lose. What difference would it make in her life if his friends rejected her? Since when hadn't they rejected her? He had already made a statement, with that one fluid motion of his arm—had said he was with her. And the people at that table could either accept her or push him out.

She didn't want that—didn't want to come between him and his friends.

Beth lifted her head, then swept around the table's end and sat down. Right beside Pepe.

Salva's throat almost closed. He wanted to rush over, pick her up, and relocate her next to the far more adaptable Tosa. Pepe might eat her for lunch. But she was god-awful brave. Salva sat down across from her, the only seat left on that end of the table.

Vaguely, he was aware that the noise in the rest of the cafeteria had risen again, but it didn't matter. Because his best friend was looking at him. Eyebrows arched, mouth quirked, as if to say, *Are you serious, man?*

Salva met the look head-on. *I'm serious. You rip her up; I'll flatten you.* He'd wasted three-quarters of the year realizing what Beth meant to him, and now that he knew, he wasn't going to deny it. What he didn't know was how his friends would react. Would they hurt her? Would they betray the half a lifetime of friendship he had built with them? He wasn't sure. After all the time he'd spent protecting this friendship, maybe it wasn't as strong as he had always tried to believe. It couldn't be if the guys would throw him out because he wanted to spend time with a girl who didn't fit into their world.

Into anyone's world.

Except she did. Not like a puzzle piece attached to his side, but like a part of his soul that had always been within him.

There was no way he could expect the guys to realize that. Or to understand that one slam, one rude comment was going tear something Salva couldn't count on being repaired.

"Sssssso," Tosa broke the barrier, "I guess you all had an eventful break. Thought you were grounded, man." He elbowed Salva.

"I was," Salva replied, "since last Sunday afternoon." *Papá* had not been too keen on his son's disappearance from the barbecue.

Beth's eyes flew up, then down, her face turning red as she opened her chocolate milk.

"D'ja tell him your news yet, Pep?" Tosa asked.

News?

"He got the scholarship," Tosa said. "For football. At Regional."

Salva couldn't hold back the grin. "Of course he did. Their defense sucks."

Pepe tossed an orange at his best friend's head.

Salva dodged.

And Pepe grinned back. "Man, you oughta be careful. That's our future alma mater you're talkin' about."

"Whoop!" Salva gave him a high five. He wasn't messing with his best friend's illusions today. Plus, Salva didn't *know* that he himself wasn't going to Regional. He hadn't heard yet from any place better.

"Congratulations, Pepe," Beth said softly.

Char broke into the conversation, sarcasm ripping through her voice. "Yes, Pepe. Congratulations." Her stare traveled coolly from Beth to Salva.

What was up with that? He'd overlooked the threat from Char. Been too worried about his friends' reactions to worry about hers. But he should have thought—should have remembered that slam on homecoming.

Suddenly, there came a movement in the periphery of his vision, followed by a clatter. And then Luka and Nalani were sitting at the far end of the table. Beth's gaze, a look of pure gratitude, went straight to her best friend.

Pepe rolled his eyes to the ceiling. *Which meant what?* That he and his iced-over girlfriend weren't hanging out here while Table Numero Uno was consumed by a bunch of nerds? Pepe lowered his fork, balancing the plastic tines on the central arch of his tray, then aimed a loaded comment at Beth: "That was a hell of a scene the two of you put on last week, sticking it to Markham."

She answered the linebacker without blinking. "Markham is an idiot. He's afraid of anything that makes him sweat."

Pepe arched an eyebrow, then concurred. "True." He turned toward Salva. "Man, Resendez, I bet Markham was wettin' his pants at the thought you might defy him in public. You know, if you'd refused to follow him down to his little office, we'd have had a revolt *rrreal*."

"He said he could yank my spot as president," said Salva.

"BS." Pepe pounded the table with the flat of his hand. "Everybody here knows you're the head of this school. We'd tear this place apart if he tried to pull that garbage. Wouldn't we?"

Tosa popped a bag of chips between his palms. "No doubt, man. Shoot, we'd show up with signs and protest songs, a couple hundred kids sittin' outside Markham's office. He'd cave in less than twenty minutes."

"Less than five if he had to hear you sing, Tos." Pepe smirked.

"I'll second that," Luka added.

Linette was nodding, and even Nalani was grinning. Which didn't make any sense.

"Don't be ridiculous." Salva dismissed the claim. "Nobody's gonna put their future on the line for me."

"Shut that." Pepe held up a hand. "I'm tellin' you, Resendez, the kids at this school would do whatever you asked. Even Markham knows that, doesn't he, Juliet?"

Beth was looking straight at Salva. "Yes," she said without hesitation.

The hand of the linebacker clapped down on her shoulder. "That's my girl."

Salva didn't even bother to argue.

16

THE TRAP

PRINCETON UNIVERSITY. Salva's heart beat hard as he stared at the professional black font inscribed in the corner of the envelope. The package was heavy, almost as thick as his thumb. He dropped the rest of the mail on the post office counter, then turned and shredded the seal.

Congratulations.

God. He'd gotten in.

Now his hands were trembling. Which wasn't okay. It had been a dare. It hadn't meant anything. The cover letter fell to the floor as he tried to flip the page. He scanned the next sheet.

Eligible for work study.

Well, duh.

Another page. *Five thousand.* A five-thousand-dollar scholarship per year. It would have paid his way at Regional. At a place like Princeton, it was nothing.

He flipped through the rest of the packet. Housing data. A catalogue. *Worthless.*

At least he'd been accepted.

Doesn't matter.

He retrieved the fallen page and crammed it along with the others back into the envelope, then gathered the mail and headed for Char's. The puddles from the morning had dried, but he wasn't grateful. He should still have been at school, waiting for Beth and their study session, but apparently Markham had instilled his paranoia into the rest of the staff. The drama teacher had pulled the plug on Beth's access to the multipurpose room.

"We can study in the library tomorrow after school," Beth had suggested, and Salva had shrugged his agreement. It would mean dealing with an audience, but well—he'd pretty much taken care of the shock factor at lunch today.

Announcement made; bulletin posted; moving on.

The guys had been cool.

Everyone had been cool—except Char.

Salva swung through her back door. The sibs were in the living room. He could hear Talia and Casandra, over the TV, engaged in one of their endless battles with Renaldo about whether girls were smarter than boys. If Char had any desire to preserve her mental health, she'd be as far away as possible.

He found her in the kitchen, crouched down, her head buried in the cupboard beneath the sink. For the first time he'd seen all year, she was out of display mode, wearing a pair of old jeans and a T-shirt. At her side was a row of cleaning supplies, an empty garbage can, and a tub of peanut butter.

"*Hola,*" he said.

Her head thudded against the top of the cupboard, then slowly she withdrew, aiming the same steely glare at him as the one she had sent at lunch. "You're early," she accused, stripping off a pair of rubber gloves.

He set the mail down on the kitchen table, then nodded at the stuff on the floor. "This looks ambitious."

"Mice," she replied.

Right. "Look, we need to talk," he said.

"Since when do we talk?"

She had a point. The year they'd dated, after *Mamá's* death, he had wanted someone to distract him from what he'd been feeling. But Char's silences hadn't worked, and he was still paying the price for asking her out. No one else should have to pay it. "Beth doesn't need any crap from you."

"Excuse me." Charla plucked a package from the counter, then ripped apart the plastic and removed a mousetrap. "If you want to mess around with the walking disaster area, that's your problem."

He cringed at the moniker. His fault. He must have referred to Beth that way at some point in front of Char.

She added, "*I'm* with Pepe."

"So I thought." Which made her sarcasm at lunch totally uncalled for. "Though if you can't even tell your mom who you're dating, you might want to slow things down."

"Oh, *that* is rich." She stuck a knife in the peanut butter and smeared the brown substance on the catch of the trap, then pulled up the wire bar, her hand vibrating from the effort.

"Look, I don't know what you think," he said, "but Pepe's going to college next year. And he's not the type to stick around if he makes a mistake."

The bar sprang loose with a nasty snap. "You're just an awesome friend, aren't you?" she mocked.

"*Claro.*" Salva removed the trap from her grasp and set it. She had no *idea* how hard it was risking his copacetic relationship with his best friend in order to give her a reality check. Why? *Why* did he feel compelled to warn her? He supposed it had something to do with *la familia*. With all those years of being her protective shield.

"You think I want to hold him back?" Her voice wavered. "You think I wouldn't *love* to get out of this town. To be free of these stupid remedial courses! Go to art school or study fashion. But you and I both know I'll be lucky if I even find a job as a beautician."

Salva stared at her. It had never occurred to him that the reason she never mentioned her dreams was because they were impossible—that for her, with a learning disability and illegal status, even Community was like Princeton.

"You think I don't know he's leaving?" She shoved the trap under the cupboard. "You're *all* leaving. I know the score, Salva." She closed the cupboard door, her hand holding it tight. "It's Pepe who doesn't have the full picture."

Her next words knifed through his chest. "You know he's under the impression the two of you are going to spend the next four years together."

Salva froze.

Slowly, Char removed the trap from his hand. "You think it's easy?" she murmured. "Knowing someone else has more choices?"

No. It wasn't easy. None of it was easy. For an instant he considered telling her about the Princeton letter and his failure to earn an adequate scholarship. Char, of all people, knew what it was like to fail.

He remembered the day he'd first met her, sitting in the dirt for hours on end in the shade under a pickup while their parents worked harvest. He'd creamed her in tic-tac-toe about fifty times. She hadn't complained. Hadn't sneaked away or thrown dirt in his face or griped about being stuck there with him.

She had not complained this year either. Not once.

He owed her, Salva realized, for taking care of his sisters. Yeah, their parents had made the arrangements, but it was Char who was stuck two days a week scrubbing cupboards and cooking real food and putting up with the same squabbling as he did. She knew what it was like to sacrifice for *la familia*.

They both knew.

But she didn't have an out.

She didn't have the promise of next fall to rescue her.

He could not tell her his problems. It wouldn't be fair. "Look, thanks for watching over Talia and Casandra," he said.

"You should tell Pepe," she insisted.

What? That I'd rather go somewhere else but might get stuck at the same school as him?

Salva reached for another trap and set it. "I'll tell him when I know something."

"You should tell him *now.*"

He scooped up the mail from the table, then turned and yelled, "Talia! Casandra! We're leaving!" He didn't wait for their response. Just swung out the back door. And ditched the Princeton envelope in the outside trash.

17

RUSH

Beth was late for her first study "date" in the library—waylaid by her own nerves, the fact that she had forgotten her book of sonnets in trig, and by the bizarre experience of having classmates speak to her who had never spoken to her in their entire career at Liberty. The disaster that was her life had been replaced by a strange realm in which her name was the one being whispered up and down the halls. And in which, during lunch that day, Pepe Real had swapped his M&M's trail mix for her chocolate milk. *Surreal.*

She ducked beneath a drooping crepe paper border in the doorway, then scanned the inside of the library. Salva was sitting at a rectangular table by the window, his back to her, sunlight gleaming on his dark hair. Was this a date? Or a study session? And how would she know the difference? What would he expect from her? Was she supposed to turn into a vapid, giggling study partner?

Vapidity was not in Beth's repertoire.

She adjusted her grip on the book she'd retrieved from trig. Then approached.

He didn't notice her. His torso was bent over an open volume as he scribbled notes on a piece of paper. The Mercenary had assigned everyone to select a sonnet and relate it to their own lives.

Beth peered over his shoulder and recognized the Shakespearean poem on the left-hand page. "My Mistress' Eyes Are Nothing Like the Sun." "You're using *that?*" she asked.

He snapped the book shut, slid his chair slightly at an angle, and grinned. "Don't worry about the sonnet. It's fine."

Fine? He was fine with relating his life and, therefore, his relationship with Beth to Shakespeare's most derisive love poem? The entire poem was about how flawed the girl was.

He folded the page of notes and tucked it inside the book, then slid the tome aside. "We have two weeks for that assignment. Let's drill for the quiz on literary terms."

Lines from the derisive sonnet flared in her mind.

Coral is far more red than her lips' red . . .

If hair be wires, black wires grow on her head . . .

I grant I never saw a goddess go . . .

Beth rounded the table, then sank into a chair across from him. Obviously, she wasn't a *goddess*, but—

"Literary terms, Beth." He waved his hand in front of her

face. "Are you here?" He opened his folder and yanked out four pages of typed notes with vocab definitions.

Clearly, as far as Salva was concerned, this was a study session. *Not* a date.

She gathered herself and plunged into quizzing him on *antagonist, antithesis,* and *allusion.* What had she expected? She didn't know the first thing about being someone's girlfriend. How romantic had she thought an hour in the library was going to be? She'd been studying with him all year. Why would this afternoon be any different?

But at the end of the hour, he carried her book to her locker.

Then slid his arm around her waist.

And guided her out the back door of the school. He paused there, his eyes flicking toward the bleachers on the football field, where members of the track team, including his best friend, were hanging out.

She prepared to stumble through a good-bye.

But the arm stayed around her waist.

And Salva walked her down the asphalt path and across the street.

He's going to escort me home.

Panic slammed into her torso, her mind reeling through all the reasons he should *not* walk her home: the clothes all over the floor, dishes on the counter, papers, books, her mother's AA materials—

Get a grip, Beth. He doesn't have to come in.

The weeds outside the trailer. Blankets instead of blinds at the windows. The dented walls of her tin-can residence.

Don't be stupid, Beth. If he knows where you live, he already knows what it looks like.

His arm moved from her waist, his fingers threading through hers. Then he ran his thumb along the inside of her palm.

God. Beth sucked in her breath. She didn't know how to do this. Her tongue, which had worked well enough five minutes ago when she had ripped apart his definition of *tautology*, ceased to function.

Please, please, *don't let me make a mistake.* What was it she had told him that day in the park? Admitting she had been afraid he would never notice her. And now that he had, her sense of inadequacy was ten times worse. How would she ever measure up to Char Mendoza? Or the other girls he had dated? Before the performance in the cafeteria, Beth had never even seriously kissed a guy. Not that that had been a problem in the park. At least it hadn't appeared to be one. But sooner or later he was bound to discover her ineptitude.

He didn't seem to mind her silence. Or to feel compelled to improve on it.

They walked without speaking for almost four blocks, doubt swirling in a blur within her head. Then he stepped off the street and started winding through a weed-covered lot in front of an empty gray house. Cheatgrass and fiddleneck stretched for her ankles as he guided her around a FOR SALE sign so old the *S* had peeled away. The gray shingles on the building's side curled from age and neglect. "Salva, what are we—"

Moments later, her spine was up against the back of the building, his hands on her waist. His mouth on hers.

Dear God, this didn't happen, did it? You didn't spend your whole life crushing on the same guy and then suddenly find him crushing right back. "Salva," she blurted. "I know I shouldn't have to ask. But are we . . . metaphorically speaking, are we . . . ?"

"Dating?" he murmured, dropping his forehead to her own. "Yeah."

Okay, that was good to confirm.

Again his mouth came down to hers.

Aren't we supposed to go out first? To places like the movie theater and the pizza parlor? Not that there were any in this town. But there were rules, weren't there? "Um . . ." she stammered. "Isn't this kind of . . . fast?"

"No." He buried his head in her T-shirt. "I should have asked you out last fall."

Last fall?

He met her gaze, then tangled his fingers within her hair. "'I never saw that you did painting need,'" he whispered. "'And therefore to your fair no painting set.'"

The sonnet. Her stomach flipped.

"'I found, or thought I found, you did exceed,'" he continued.

"'The barren tender of a poet's debt.'" Only it wasn't the sonnet she had thought he was working on. He leaned in close and whispered against her ear. "'And therefore have I slept in your report.'"

She was caught. Totally and completely snagged.

"'How far a modern quill doth come too short'"—his thumb traced her cheek—"'speaking of worth . . .'"

She forgot where she was. Forgot what she was doing. Forgot everything except that thumb edging its way along her skin.

"'This silence for my sin you did impute.'"

The hell with movies.

His thumb slid to the bottom of her lip. "'There lives more life in one of your fair eyes than both your poets'"—his dark gaze glanced up toward heaven—"'can in praise devise.'"

And the hell with pizza.

She kissed him, living and reliving a thousand dreams. Rules didn't matter. What mattered was that *he* was interested in kissing *her*. And she had never been interested in kissing anyone else.

When he broke away, she wasn't anywhere near ready for the separation.

"Beth"—he still had his hands in her hair—"the truth is I've been thinking about this forever. Since homecoming."

Five months *definitely* wasn't forever. But she understood now why that first kiss in the park had been so intense. Because for so long they'd both been denying their feelings. She bit her lip, glanced down at the weeds, then confessed. "Salva, I've been imagining this since the *eighth* grade."

He pulled upright, staring at her.

Maybe the admission had been *too* pathetic.

"Well, not all that time," she amended. "It's just I had a huge crush on you that year, and I kept *waiting* for you to notice me, which I know was stupid, but—"

"Don't say that." His eyebrows furrowed. "You aren't stupid, Beth. You're one of the most intelligent people I know." He thrust his hands in his pockets, then shook his head slightly and took a step backward. "But eighth grade . . . I never . . . I barely remember that year." He took another step, then turned and began heading toward the street.

If she was so smart, why was he pulling away?

"You don't forget anything," she challenged, following him along the side of the building, through the weeds. *Not calc formulas or deadlines or details on the periodic table.*

"That's not what I . . ." He reached the road. "It's not about memory. It's . . . my life . . . what happened."

What had happened? Beth skidded on loose pavement as she struggled to sort through the conversation.

He picked up his pace, walking so fast she would have assumed he was rejecting her except he kept heading toward her home.

But then he turned.

Which wasn't needed. The fastest way to the Courant trailer was straight ahead through the cemetery.

His life. In the eighth grade.

His mother had died that fall.

How could he say Beth wasn't stupid? She had known. Of course she had known. His loss of his mother was one of the reasons Beth had been drawn to him. Though when she was thirteen, she hadn't understood. Because back then *she* hadn't lost anyone. She had felt sorry for him, yes. Had thought it was terrible that someone their age might lose a parent to cancer. But she had *not* fathomed, at the time, how it must have impacted him. To have a person he loved, maybe the person he loved more than anyone else, maybe the person who loved *him* more than anyone else—suddenly gone. Absent.

"Salva..." She caught his elbow. He hadn't been running from her. He was running away from that loss. She *did* understand now. "If you ever want to talk about that year . . . about your mother . . ."

He shuddered. "I-I'm sorry . . . I just can't."

This time Beth was the one to take his hand. "It's okay," she whispered. Though it wasn't. It wasn't okay if he still couldn't bring himself to visit his mother's grave four and a half years after her death.

Salva couldn't seem to hang on to anything. April was like a time warp, sucking him in at the beginning and spitting him out at the end. Every minute blitzed by. Tosa was scheduled to fly out for basic training the week after graduation. Pepe had pre-season practice in July and was talking about going down in June if he could find a place. And Beth?

Salva's relationship with Beth was like drowning. Their time together was never enough. Either for homework—he'd somehow drawn the massive job of attorney for the defense in the upcoming mock trial for cit/gov—or for her. He snagged every minute he could alone with her, usually behind the abandoned building on their walk home. But as soon as they touched, they were kissing, and then it would be time for her to leave or for him to pick up his sisters.

She deserved better: chocolate or jewelry or a real date, but he didn't have any money. Talia had come home from school with a note saying she needed glasses. Even if he had had the cash, he didn't have transportation to take Beth out. Doubling with Pepe and Char was about as appealing a thought as sitting through another one of *Papá*'s lectures.

At the end of the month, though, Linette threw another party. Salva wanted to go because he didn't know how many more chances he was going to get with all the people who mattered. Including Beth. Who wasn't interested in coming. So Salva invited Luka. Who invited Nalani. Who begged her best friend to come as her own social support.

Which meant Beth arrived at the party at eight o'clock, her hair all swirled on top of her head and twined with a pink ribbon Salva was sure wasn't hers. And which he had an instinctive desire to remove. But there was also a look on her face—a look he was certain, even from clear across Linette's family room, had nothing to do with the salsa music or flowing alcohol or couples dancing in the middle of the floor.

She blew right through them, engulfing him in a fierce hug. "I got in!" she shouted over the music.

He didn't have to ask—didn't have to question or wonder or doubt. He knew instantly that she'd been accepted at Stanford. And it wasn't a surprise. At some point in the middle of knowing her, he had come to believe she could do anything. "I knew it!" he shouted back.

And she looked up, laughing. "You are such a liar, Salva Resendez!"

But he wasn't lying. And he wasn't upset, though he had been during the previous week when he'd had to throw away his most recent acceptance letter—Harvard this time. Her face was alive, her eyes shining, the joy bursting from them. She deserved to go where she wanted. And she wanted the best.

He wouldn't have needed her if she hadn't.

Beth wasn't exactly sure how they wound up in the storage room. She'd been careful not to enter a bedroom with Salva, either here at the party or anywhere else over the past four weeks, though it had helped that the trailer was such a mess she'd have died of embarrassment before letting him through her own front door. But somehow, with the excitement of the acceptance letter, her defenses had lulled.

And now here she was, in the dark, with only the flicker of the electric furnace to shed light on the fact that she was propped up against a stack of cardboard boxes, Salva's mouth on hers, his chest against her own. *His arms, his skin, his touch.*

God, it was like heaven.

His hand slid to her side, then up under her shirt.

Oh, this was not a good idea.

The sensation of that hand running up her flesh sent a thousand nerves pulsing. "No," she finally mouthed against his lips.

And the hand stopped, withdrew. "Beth, I promise I won't . . ." His voice was hoarse, pleading.

The problem was that *she* couldn't promise. When they were together, alone, everything went so fast and felt so right. She was certain if he asked for more, it would still feel right, all the way around the bases and back again. She was not going to end up like her mother. "I can't, Salva," Beth whispered.

"*Jesús.*" He said it in Spanish, then sank back into the flickering dark, his hands running through his hair. "I don't know what happens when I'm with you. I never plan. It's just—we start, and I can't quit."

Except he could. He just had.

Her breath was still coming ragged. "It's not only you," she said, "but I don't want . . . to ruin—"

"I know," he interrupted. "We both want a future, Beth. Neither of us wants to risk that." There was a pause. "Do we?"

Was he asking if she wanted to have sex?

"No," she replied, her heart speeding up as if he'd actually said the words. For a heartbeat, silence stretched between them, and then she whispered, "Do you think, though, that maybe I should go to the clinic and ask for—"

"Yes." Suddenly, he was clear across the room. "We should both get checked out and invest in protection."

Her heart was racing around the block.

"Just in case we screw up," he added.

Well, that was romantic.

Salva left the party early—around eleven P.M.—grateful for the escape. Beth had already split, right after he'd admitted that he was afraid of having sex with her. At least he'd admitted his fear to himself. Or rather how easy it would be to have sex with her. And risk wrecking his entire life. He wasn't like Pepe. If Salva messed up, he wasn't going to be able to walk away. Of course he hadn't managed to explain that to Beth. Had probably just offended her. *Good one, Resendez. Real smooth.*

For some reason his best friend, who was Salva's alibi, had wanted to get away from the party as well.

The sports car was flying down the highway at about ninety.

Salva leaned back against the leather passenger seat. "What's up, man?"

"Char."

Of course.

"She said she had a headache."

"Uh-huh."

"It's the fifth friggin' headache she's had this month."

Char had always had migraines, Salva knew, but she wasn't bad at faking them either. Maybe she'd actually listened to his advice to slow things down. His mind snagged on the irony. "Don't worry," he told his best friend. "I'm sure she's still interested."

Pepe swerved around a pickup that was probably clocking eighty. "Who's worried? I just wasn't aware we were going backward. She's all freakin' out because she bombed the state test again. As if that has anything to do with us. What's she think?"

"She's thinking she's not going with you."

Silence. Darkness swam around the headlights. There was almost nobody around here, especially at night.

Pepe took the next turnoff, one of those that didn't lead anywhere—just some scenic viewpoint. A good place to make out if you hadn't screwed your chances. The car shot to the edge of a cliff. And stopped. Then Pepe turned off the engine. "So . . . Stanford, huh?" he asked at last.

When had Beth entered this conversation?

"That's a pretty tough school," Pepe added.

Salva messed with the visor above the windshield. "She deserves it."

"She's pretty smart then."

"Yeah." He left the visor up.

"So where are *you* going?" The question hit him in the chest.

Salva turned and stared at his best friend. "What?"

Pepe was gazing out into the wide black emptiness that was the scenic view at night. "Look, Resendez, I ain't stupid. I figure if Beth Courant's getting into Stanford, then you're getting into somewhere a hell of a lot better than Regional, huh?"

Salva's hand tightened on the door. "Beth has a financial trust. I don't."

"Just be straight with me, man." His best friend's gaze turned direct. "Everybody else is talkin' about next year. You're not. Why?"

Salva rubbed the heel of his palm against the leather armrest. The car locks clicked off, then on. "I'm still waiting to hear back from State."

"State University? Is that where you want to go?"

It was the best non–Ivy League school he had applied to. "Yeah, if I can get the money."

Pepe's head fell back against his seat. "You think it's likely?"

"I don't know." Salva didn't. He'd been offered full scholarships for all the smaller, regional schools he'd applied to, but State was a definite step up.

"Didn't your brother want to go there? Before your mom—" Pepe stopped.

Salva closed his eyes. Pepe was the only one who knew to stop. He was the one who had been there the day of the funeral—the day Salva couldn't make himself attend. They'd spent the whole day together, him and the guy everyone thought was trouble. And Pepe had seen Salva cry like a baby and never told anybody.

"Miguel applied there." Salva swallowed. "He didn't get in. He was gonna go to Regional." *Before the doctor's bills for Mamá made him quit.*

"Well, it ain't a bad school," Pepe said.

"No." Salva opened his eyes. "It ain't."

His best friend grinned.

"It's just"—Salva's hand formed a fist as he tried to explain—"if I can get into State, it's gonna mean a lot, you know, to my father—"

"Shit." Pepe rolled down the front windows. "This isn't about your father. It's about you, always having to win. You're such an f-ing competitor."

The comment made no sense. "You're the one with the sports scholarship," Salva argued.

"No, man." Pepe pulled the keys from the ignition. "I'm just the only one of us willing to *settle* for the sports scholarship. You were all-state. You could have played at Regional, but that's not enough for you. You're gonna go conquer the friggin' world." He held up his hand, car keys dangling in his palm. "And that's okay, 'cause when you do, you're gonna remember tonight, and who let you drive, huh?"

Oh yeahhh.

18

SUCH STUFF AS DREAMS ARE MADE ON

Bang! Salva looked up, annoyed, from the arc of interview notes he'd spread out on the kitchen table. It sucked to have homework on a Saturday evening; but the party had been last night, and he now had less than forty-eight hours to prepare for the mock trial on Monday. Lucia, who was home yet again, had *claimed* she was taking the girls for a walk to help her order dinner at the *taquería* downtown. But the front door had just slammed.

Señor Resendez arrived in the kitchen, breathing hard, and grinning from one end of his face to the other. He lifted an envelope in his hand. "From the State University!"

Salva eyed the package. It was thick, but he'd been fooled by that before, with the trashed acceptance from Princeton.

Papá thrust the envelope into his hands. "Open!"

Trying not to let the package shake, Salva ripped the seal.

His father was hovering, leaning over his shoulder, hands pressed together in prayer position.

Congratulations!
You are the chosen recipient of the Joseph Bauermann
Strauss Scholarship. This award is a full four-
year scholarship for State's nationally recognized
engineering program.

"What does it say?" *Papá* was now holding his clenched hands over his head.

"It . . ." Salva struggled for breath. *Don't tell him until you're sure.* His father's trembling had turned into an earthquake. Salva scanned the rest of the letter. "It says I've been accepted and that . . ." It was *real*. He was going to State. A flood of relief washed through him. "They're going to pay my whole way."

The hands exploded. *"¿Todo?"*

"All the tuition, not my books or housing, but—"

"You can stay with Miguel!" his father shouted. "You can work for your books!"

Then the arms were around Salva in a huge, crushing hug. *"Mijo, mijo,"* his father repeated over and over again. *My son. My son.* The words brought tears onto Salva's face. But there was no shame. His father wouldn't see them anyway, because the dampness soaking Salva's shirt wasn't his. Those tears were his father's, and Salva knew, for the first time, the unbelievable feeling of making someone else's dream come true.

———

When the girls came home, Lucia consigned the tacos to the fridge and cooked instead. They had enchiladas with mole sauce, roasted peppers, and fried ice cream. Talia and Casandra took turns hugging Salva, possibly because they were happy for him, but more likely in thanks for the food.

Dinner was followed by the longest string of phone calls Salva had ever participated in in his life. Grandparents, both sets; his aunts and uncles; and three million cousins, spread out everywhere from Guanajuato to San Antonio to North Carolina. Of course his father did most of the talking. Salva just had to get on the phone to listen to the congratulations. He didn't even know a fraction of the people who gave him *felicidades*, but he could hear how happy his father was every time he had the chance to tell someone his son was going to a four-year state university.

After passing the phone back to *Papá* for the umpteenth time, Salva sneaked into the kitchen, poured himself a mug of cinnamon hot chocolate, and dropped with fake exhaustion into a chair.

Lucia laughed, shaking the remnants of dishwater from her fingers, then reached for a towel. "Are you going to let *Papá* do all the calling?" she teased. "You know he could go on all night."

Salva shrugged, his excitement about telling his best friend tempered by the knowledge that deep down Pepe would be disappointed. "I'll see Pepe and Tosa tomorrow at church."

"And what about your girlfriend?"

There was no way Salva was letting his father listen in on

that conversation. Plus, Beth had said she and Nalani were spending the rest of the weekend somewhere out of town. "I'll see Beth on Monday."

"Ah!" Lucia swatted him with the towel. "Then you are dating the girl who is okay pretty."

"Diga." Their father stepped through the doorway, making his son jump. But *Papá* just handed over the phone for the hundredth time.

Salva pressed it to his ear.

"Hola, little brother. So I'm told you're coming to live with me."

Miguel. Salva almost dropped the phone. *Papá* had called Miguel? After all this time? His father had said something before, but Salva hadn't taken it seriously.

"Un momento." Salva eased past his father, shook his head at Lucia's questioning look, and left the kitchen. Then shut himself in his room—the same room he had shared for the first six years of his life with the person on the other end of the phone.

"Congratulations," said Miguel.

"Um . . . *hola,"* Salva managed.

"You know my place is only a half hour's city bus ride from your new school. Are you coming to stay with me, or what?"

"Well . . ." Salva didn't want to take anything more from his brother. Ever. Miguel had derailed his entire life to help support his younger siblings. And had ultimately lost *la familia* in the process. Or maybe not. Maybe Salva could make up for that now. "If I get a job, I might be able to pay you rent."

"You won't have time for a job. Not if you're going into engineering at State."

Salva hadn't thought much about the program. He'd written his college essay about becoming an engineer because it was the most high-profile degree offered at the school. And because the lady who'd run the scholarship workshop at Liberty had said you should always pick a career, to make the essay more convincing. But the program *was* supposed to be intense. "Well, maybe some of the local scholarships will help cover the cost of a place to stay," he said, running his hand over a crack in the wall. Miguel had started to putty it up once, but ants still came through it in the summer.

"Don't be silly, Salva. You know I owe you."

That was stupid. Why would Miguel owe him?

"Don't lie to me," Salva said. He didn't need his brother acting like he hadn't sacrificed anything.

"What?"

Salva pressed his thumb into the crack, just above the plaster. "It should have been you first at a four-year college. I know you quit to help support us. It wasn't fair. I'll pay you back somehow. I don't know when but—"

"*Hermano,* I had enough of school. You've gotta know that. You heard the fights."

Yeah, Salva had heard them. He'd heard Miguel shouting that his work wasn't appreciated. That his paycheck was what put food on the table. And *Papá* had yelled back that he could take care of his own *familia*. And that he didn't need a dropout for a son. *What had that meant, exactly?* Salva had assumed, at the time, that his father had been exaggerating. Trying to ignore reality in order to live up to the promise he had made *Mamá* about all her children getting an education.

"You're overthinking this, aren't you?" Miguel's voice broke through Salva's thoughts. "Look, I left you in the lurch with *Papá*, let you take on all his big dreams so that I could move to the city and work construction. You know it, and I know it. And, listen, hey, it wasn't fair. We both know that, too."

The plaster beneath Salva's thumb began to crumble.

"But that doesn't mean I don't want you around, little brother. Just because I couldn't handle all the pressure of *Papá's* expectations doesn't mean I'm not just as happy for you as he is. Of course you're staying here. And I'm really proud of you, okay?"

Salva didn't know what to say—didn't know how to deal with what he was hearing. That his brother had *chosen* not to return to school. Had left it unfinished. *Like he left everything unfinished—the paint job on the front door, the putty in this stupid crack.*

Salva's mind reeled through that awful year. His mother's death. His father's grief. And then, sometime in the spring, *Papá's* announcement that he had been promoted to manager and that

199

his older son could start working his way back to school. Miguel had asserted that *la familia* couldn't really afford it.

And Salva had believed him.

Had blamed *Papá* for the fights.

"Okay?" Miguel repeated.

No, it wasn't okay. Salva had *needed* his older brother that year. The least, the *least* Miguel could have done was to brave their father's anger and pick up the phone. "Look, thanks for the offer," Salva said, then let the signal die.

He leaned back and closed his eyes, the blood in his veins replaced by disillusionment. His brother had dropped out because of the pressure? What kind of an excuse was that?

Salva understood pressure. The obligation to prove that his parents' decision to sacrifice everything to come here hadn't been wasted. That he could excel. Could learn as well as all the other American kids. That he could beat them at their own game. A fiery burn pulsed through his stomach—that same intense feeling that had wound its way through his gut every time he'd called a play during the state-championship final. That need to win.

Pepe had been right. It wasn't just about *Papá*.

Salva's father might be seriously high-stress. Might misread people like Beth and Markham and Miguel. But *Papá* was right about Salva. Education was his way out. And on this point, this one basic elemental point, the two of them were in complete agreement. Slowly, Salva straightened, then stepped outside the room, returning the phone to his father, and said with more conviction than he ever had in his life, "*Gracias, Papá.*"

His friends' reactions to the scholarship news didn't quite rival his family's, but Tosa gave Salva a huge flying chest butt that made the *abuelas* at church gasp. And Pepe delivered a high five and a fist pump that his best friend knew was sincere.

Still, Salva found the wait to tell Beth tougher than he had anticipated. He walked by her trailer Sunday evening, but the lights were out and nothing at all seemed to be moving. So he reconciled himself to wait. All night, through the delay of walking his sisters to the bus, then out on the front steps by the main entrance of the high school. For thirteen minutes.

She finally arrived with about five minutes to spare before the bell. He grabbed her by the hands, tugged her behind the hedge along the building front, and watched her face as he talked.

"Engineering?" she repeated when he finished.

"Yes." He pulled her farther into the crevice between the gray wall and half-brown shrubs, then reiterated his explanation. "It's a *full* scholarship."

She wasn't jumping. Or hugging him. Or even looking like she was trying to look happy. "Why would you want a scholarship for engineering?" she asked.

His jaw clenched. She wasn't going to do this. She wasn't seriously going to turn into the type of person who cut you off just when you were getting your dreams. Was she? "Because it's *State* University," he said. "It's a four-year scholarship. It means they'll pay my way."

"Of course they'll pay your way. All the state colleges that replied to you so far have agreed to pay your way."

Yeah, but the others were minor regional schools. This was a major university.

The first bell rang, followed by the sounds of multiple pairs of feet sprinting past the hedge and heading for the main door. He should go, but he just couldn't leave it like this. Of all the people in the school, he'd been counting on her to understand.

Beth dropped her backpack from her shoulder. "Salva, since when have you planned on becoming an engineer?"

"I'm taking AP calc," he stated the obvious. "Advanced physics. Science and math; they're what I'm good at."

"You're good at everything"—the backpack fell from her elbow into the dirt—"even AP English, if you're strong enough to say what you really think. I've never heard you talk about wanting to design roads or structures or buildings."

"Well, we can't all write romance novels." The slam came out of his mouth without permission.

She jolted. For a second, he thought he saw her wince, but her tone hardened. "You are a coward."

"For going into the toughest program in the state?" He could feel the anger building within his chest.

She was giving him that look—the same one she'd given

him last fall when she'd ripped apart his paper on Milton. That blunt, baffled, I-thought-you-were-better-than-this look. "You're going to take this scholarship," she accused, "because it's the best one they've offered you, and to hell with what you want."

"I want this!" he shouted, not caring if anyone heard.

"No, you don't."

"It's a four-year university. At the best school in the state. In one of the best programs out there. *That* is what I want."

"It's not enough."

She was impossible!

"Look!" he shouted, "I'm sorry I can't afford one of your Ivy League colleges!"

She backed away, slightly. He hadn't told her about the responses from Princeton and Harvard. He guessed he should have. Then maybe she would have understood.

Her voice softened. "It's not about the school, Salva." She reached out as if to touch his arm. "Or which program is the best. It's about what you want to do with your life."

He swept her hand away. "This *is* what I want—"

"Engineering?" Her arms came across her chest. "You don't have any passion for engineering."

Just like that. She said it as if she was reciting some fact he had failed to study for a final.

And the statement drove home. Direct.

Because she was right.

19

PASSION

"I . . ." Salva stammered. "I'm not passionate about anything," which, really, on a scale of one to ten, was a zero on the list of things he should ever have said to Beth.

She winced.

The bell rang.

They were both late for cit/gov. Salva ran. *There's nothing wrong with not knowing what I want to do,* he told himself. *Isn't that kind of the point of my first year of college? Taking the stuff I don't have a chance to take at Liberty?*

He could already hear Beth's argument. *And how are you going to do that if you tie yourself to an engineering program?*

"You're late, counselor." Coach Robson held up a penalty flag as Salva entered cit/gov, which had been transformed into a courtroom: Robson's desk as the judge's bench, the audience at the back, a chair for the witness stand, a desk and computer for the court reporter's table, a row of seats for the jury box. And two sets of desks, separated by an aisle, for the lawyers.

Salva hurried to the nearest one and dumped his stuff: four books, three folders, three notebooks, and his pen. He hadn't had time to put away anything or visit his locker, but his plan for the trial was here. In this pile. Somewhere.

A whistle sailed from the back of the room, followed by Pepe's voice. "Looks like the counsel for the defense was engaging in a little unprofessional activity with the court reporter."

Which meant Beth had arrived.

Salva avoided her gaze as she brushed past him en route to the reporter's table.

Coach Robson had launched into a lecture for the jury members. Phrases glided back: "Jury of peers . . . burden of proof . . . beyond reasonable doubt."

"Salva, are you listening?" Char asked at his side. There were real lines under her eyes. Maybe the headaches Pepe had mentioned had been real. Or maybe she was just freaking out about speaking in public.

"Yeah," he lied. "I've got this. Don't worry. You aren't going to have to take the stand." He found his cit/gov notebook and flipped it open.

Slam! Luka was standing across the aisle, a fist on his desk, the other hand pointing at Char. "This woman has committed a crime, an affront to all the students of Liberty High." He rounded the edge of the prosecutor's area and swept in front of the entire row of jury members. "We were all injured when she *stole*"—he whirled and pointed at the blue-and-gold object on Robson's desk—"the *torch* of Liberty High."

Ill-smothered laughter came from the back. Most people thought the torch was a stupid mascot.

But Salva had to hand it to Luka. The guy was dynamic.

The running back snagged an empty chair from the jury box and propped his foot on it, then faced the entire audience. "The prosecution will prove that Char Mendoza plotted the taking of the torch and committed the act by herself and of her own free will. How is it we know this?" The foot came off the chair. Because"— Luka began to pace—"the defendant was *seen* stealing the mascot." Turn. "The mascot was found in *her* locker." Turn. "And as if this were not enough, she *confessed* to the crime." His hands lifted to the air. "Can there be a more cut-and-dried case? Ladies and gentlemen of the jury"—he bowed in their direction—"I think not."

The audience applauded. It was hard to blame them.

Salva waited for renewed silence to create its own emphasis. Then he stood and spoke calmly. "The defense will disprove *all* of the prosecutor's claims. We argue that Miss Mendoza is not the criminal here, but the victim."

"Oh no, man. She's goin' *down*!" Pepe shouted from the back.

Coach Robson picked up his gavel. "Real, you are out of order."

Yeah, Pepe, you just wait your turn. "My client"—Salva opened his palm toward Char—"did not set out to commit a crime against Liberty. She was coerced, by one of the very people whose job it is to defend the law. And then she was denied

the basic rights ensured her as a member of this society. We"—
he nodded at the jury—"must correct this flaw and dismiss all
charges."

No applause, but he could hear the murmurs ripple through
the room.

Luka was grinning. "Forget it, man," he whispered across
the aisle as Salva sat down. "The defense *never* wins in mock
trials."

Char was biting a fingernail.

"Relax," Salva told her. "We have a case." *A damn fine one.*

Luka called his first witness, Tosa, who came up wearing a
bright blue costume version of a policeman's hat. "Officer Tosa,"
Luka addressed him. "Can you describe for us what happened
on the day of the arrest?"

Tosa straightened the hat and spoke: "Well, my partner"—
Pepe let out a whoop—"told me he'd seen Char steal the torch.
So he distracted her while I raided her locker." Tosa drummed
a rhythm on his knees. "And *found* the torch."

"Then what happened?" Luka was bouncing on the balls of
his feet.

"Pepe told her she was under arrest." Tosa smirked. "Which
didn't go over too well. She called him a—"

"I don't think that's necessary." Coach Robson tapped his
gavel.

"Well," Tosa said, "she called him a pretty foul name, then
sorta slumped against her locker and admitted we caught her."

"Did she confess to the crime?" Luka stopped bouncing.

"I asked if she admitted to stealing the torch, and she said, 'Yes, now get out my face!'"

Luka whirled, snapped his fingers, and stepped down. "Your witness."

Salva stood at his seat. "Officer Tosa, did you see the crime being committed?"

"Nope. But I was there when the torch was *found*!" Tosa pumped a fist.

"And did you have a warrant for searching Miss Mendoza's locker?"

"Um . . ." Tosa flipped the brim of his hat to one side and glanced toward Pepe. "Maybe my partner got one."

Sure he did. "And did you read Miss Mendoza her Miranda rights before hearing her confession?"

"Umm . . ." The hat popped off and rolled behind the chair.

There was a low growl from Luka. *Poor guy.* Should have prepped his witness.

Salva clarified: "Did either you or your partner tell Miss Mendoza she had the right to remain silent?"

A light went on in Tosa's eyes, followed by a sudden cringe. "Well . . . no." He reached down and retrieved the hat. "But the torch was right there in her locker, man."

"Judge Robson," Salva said, "I move that the witness's testimony about Miss Mendoza's confession be stricken from the record."

"Motion granted," the judge concurred.

"I have no further questions for this witness." Salva sat down.

Luka tossed an eraser at him, then called up Pepe.

Who strode forward bearing a lined piece of paper with the word *Warrant* scrawled across it. *No doubt written thirty seconds ago.* When he and Tosa crossed paths, Pepe snagged his partner's hat, then slid it on backward, continued to the witness chair, and sat down.

As expected, Pepe was full of BS. He claimed he had been working as an undercover agent, overheard Char admit to planning the theft, and then, due to his stealth skills, witnessed the entire heist.

This time, as Luka gave up the floor, he cast a wary eye at his opponent.

The clock on the wall gave Salva only ten minutes. He rounded the edge of his desk. "Mr. Real, can you please describe for the court your relationship with Miss Mendoza?"

That woke up the audience. Laughter engulfed the room.

"How much of a description do you want?" Pepe said, feeding the laughter. *Good.* That was what Salva needed—Pepe the showman.

Salva's pulse began to speed. "What is your relationship to the defendant?"

"We're dating, all right. Not my fault His Honor put us on different sides of this thing."

"Move on, Resendez," said Coach.

"So, Officer Real." Salva was standing about five feet from the witness. "When your girlfriend told you, in confidence, that she had been assigned to steal the torch, *you* chose to spy on her. Is that correct?"

"Yeah." Pepe blew a green bubble with his chewing gum.

"So you didn't, as you claimed earlier, *overhear* her plotting. She actually told you her assignment, right?"

The bubble popped. "Yeah, well, like I said, it wasn't my fault."

"And did your girlfriend have a plan when she first told you about her assignment?"

"Uh . . ."

"Come on, Pep"—Salva switched to informal address. Messing with his opponent's game. "It was you who created the plan for stealing the mascot, wasn't it?"

"Objection," Luka said. "Leading the witness."

Give me a break! There was no chance Char had stolen that torch on her own.

"Overruled." said Robson.

Yes. Salva glided up to the witness chair. "Take the credit, bro, it was you who created the plan for stealing the mascot, and you who stood guard to make sure no one stopped Char when she did it, huh?" He was in the zone. Adrenaline rushed through his entire body. Pepe probably didn't even realize he was nodding. This was better than football. It took all the same skills: fake-outs and shifts and the ability to read the players.

But this wasn't about points. Salva shot a glance toward Char. It was about *people*. "In fact, Officer Real, there is no evidence that the defendant would have successfully stolen the mascot without your help, is there?"

Pepe's mouth locked on open for a couple seconds. Before he shrugged. "Yeah, all right. But I'm not the one on trial."

You should be. "The defense rests."

They were out of time. Luka was called for his closing statement and did just as dynamic a job as he had earlier. But the guy had no real argument. And Coach cut him off after three minutes.

Salva walked up to the jury. "I submit to you, ladies and gentlemen," he said, "that the defendant had no plan for the actual theft, that she acted under the leadership of the very man who arrested her, and that then she was deprived of her rights. All the significant evidence against her comes at the word of one man—a man who has demonstrated incompetence and admitted to having a personal relationship with the defendant. His actions are clearly an abuse of power. But that is another trial. This is the trial of Charla Mendoza. The burden of proof lies upon the prosecution, and there can be *no* doubt that they have not met that burden." Salva stopped, did his best to make eye contact with each of the jurors, then took his seat.

The jury pushed and shoved one another from the room.

"Do you think it worked?" Char asked. She had gnawed off the rims of two fingernails.

He had won every point. But Salva could feel his hands beginning to shake. This wasn't football. There was no scoreboard.

The jury bounded back into the room. His stomach rolled. They hadn't even taken five minutes.

"Ladies and gentlemen of the jury, do you have a verdict?" Coach Robson asked.

The entire group confirmed at once. Which led to a delay. The teacher reminded the jury members that only one person should speak on their behalf. Nobody could remember who had been selected, but someone new was finally chosen.

Salva clenched his shaking hands into fists. Luka couldn't have been right. Even a group this incompetent had to know that the case for the defense had been stronger.

The newly chosen student stood up.

Char stood as well.

Salva's chest had gone tight.

"Char Mendoza," said the jury member, "you have been found guilty on the count of theft and are sentenced to five years of fake prison."

Crap.

The room erupted. With laughter. And Pepe's and Tosa's cheers. Then the bell rang, and the entire audience jumped out of their seats. "We'll talk about it tomorrow!" Coach yelled over the noise. But no one cared. A flood of audience members rushed for the door.

Pepe emerged, slinging an arm around Char. "Tough luck, sweetheart," he said. "Nice try, Resendez."

Nice try? The whole thing sucked. How could Salva have lost? But the answer was all around him, jury members crowing about having the power.

"Hey, well argued, man," Luka said, slapping him on the back and then disappearing.

In a matter of seconds, everyone had left.

Except Beth. Who was standing near Salva. Waiting for him.

"It isn't fair," he muttered.

"No." She started gathering his things.

"But it *should* be. Justice. That's what we're supposed to be learning. The law . . . the *law* should be fair. Power should be used fairly." The whole thing felt too real. Too close to what his father was always saying about cops and why you should never let them notice you. Because if they did, you'd be the one on trial, and it'd be their word against yours.

"You're right," said Beth.

"Then why doesn't anyone else *care*?" His voice was rising, and he knew it shouldn't. "They just—they blew it all off. I *hate* it when people do that!"

"I know." She held out his books, then cocked her head and met his gaze. "Does calculus ever make you feel this passionate?"

20

AN IMMINENT EXPLOSION

Salva tried living in denial. All week. In math he tried to care about inverting functions. In science he tried to care whether the variable in his lab was dependent or independent. He would do almost anything to convince himself that he could love engineering—to preserve the pride he had heard in his father's voice last Saturday. But there was no way Salva could afford State without the engineering scholarship.

It's not about the school, Beth's words from Monday drilled into him.

And maybe it wasn't, but his father . . .

Oh God, the thought of telling *Papá* his son wanted to reject the scholarship made Salva's entire body crumble from the inside out.

By lunchtime on Friday, though, Salva knew his grasp at denial had failed. All his friends were excited, making plans for the big Cinco de Mayo party downtown that evening. But he couldn't make plans. His father would be home early, due to the holiday. And there would be time to talk.

There was no future after that.

The afternoon passed in a foggy blur. When the final bell rang, Salva dumped his physics stuff in his locker, retrieved *The Aeneid* for homework, then glared at the cover. He hated Aeneas. The guy was supposed to be a hero just for bowing to his fate. Salva dumped the book back into his locker.

He didn't want to go home.

But then Beth arrived, assuming he had stalled to walk with her. Ten minutes later he found himself stumbling into a pothole in the street.

She rescued him and continued her pace. "You're thinking with your head," she told him.

Which made no sense. The problem was he couldn't think. He wished he could.

A scratchy electronic sound came from the direction of downtown, then a few seconds of badly recorded *conjunto* music. And more scratching. Someone must be testing the sound system for the celebration.

"Most people think with their heads," Salva said, letting his fingers wind into her hair.

Another thirty seconds of accordion notes screeched from downtown.

"That's where they mess up," Beth replied, still walking.

He needed her to stop.

His hand caressed the back of her neck. "I think that's why they don't"—he lowered his voice—"mess up."

"Maybe not the small stuff." She turned to face him. "But sometimes their lives."

He knew she was right. Had known all week. But he didn't want to discuss the scholarship. Didn't want to think about the conversation that was waiting for him at home.

Instead, he tried to pull her toward the cover of a scraggly tree.

She pulled back. "Salva, you can't hide from yourself."

Why couldn't he?

"You can't decide what you are going to do based on what is logical," she insisted. "You have to *feel*."

He kissed her. Right there in the street. Deep. Her body answered, and he pulled her to him. Tight. Intense. She was the only thing between his soul and the swirling maelstrom in his stomach. Her touch was his only hope for escape. She *was* feeling. And heart. His hands clung to her shoulders. "I *feel*, Beth," he told her, then breathed her in.

Vroom. Cough! The scent of exhaust interrupted.

He jerked back, thrusting her away. Too late. He could see the green duct-taped pickup chugging past.

Beth's eyes were wide. Injured. She turned and fled around the corner.

Oh, this was great. Great! *En el nombre de Dios.* Salva sprinted after her.

She had at least a block's lead.

"Beth, would you . . . wait!"

She stumbled, and he gained ground. "Look, I'm sorry, all right? I—" His hand snagged hers.

She jerked away. "You're ashamed of me."

Ashamed? That was so far from the truth he lost his ability to argue.

"You don't want your father to know you're with me," she added.

Okay, well, that was accurate, but not because Salva was ashamed. He'd figured she was in the same situation—that neither of their parents was too keen on the whole cross-cultural thing. He regained his voice. "You haven't exactly been in a hurry to introduce me to your *mother.*"

But Beth was shaking her head—no, she was literally shaking. "That's different," she whispered. "That's . . ." She stepped backward.

What had he missed? What didn't he know? He reached for her again.

And then froze, for the first time noting the crumbling stones around her.

His entire body went hollow.

"Salva?" She was talking, but he couldn't follow her words. All he could take in were the white markers of their surroundings. The hallmarks of death.

"Salva, you're hurting me."

Hurt? That was all he was. A frozen statue of pain.

His hand lifted, and he realized she was prying her wrist from his grip. But she didn't pull away. Instead, she gently clasped the back of his hand. Maintaining touch.

Why the graveyard? How could she have run toward the graveyard?

Without permission his eyes began to scan the tombstones.

Beth eased an arm around his waist. "These are the older plots," she whispered. "The newer ones are this way."

And he let her guide him. He didn't mean to. Didn't tell his body to walk. But it moved like an empty glass being slid across a table. She curved around a central, almost gardenlike section of the cemetery, past naked rosebushes and trees by clearly grouped family plots.

Then she led him over a small rise and down. Into a shadeless grassy plain of stones.

He tried to breathe, and his chest vibrated with the effort.

Beth paused. Again his eyes scanned the stones.

But she pulled him forward past the rows. One. Two. Four. How did she know where to go?

Because she's stronger than me.

She turned him toward the eighth row.

He couldn't move.

Her hand slid up to his shoulder, the touch propelling him forward.

And there was the name, at the center of a slender tombstone etched with lilies.

AZUCENA IMELDA MUÑOZ RESENDEZ

Salva dropped to his knees in the grass. *"Mamá."* His voice broke, then flowed into solid Spanish. Apologizing. It all spilled out: his confusion about the future, the need to reject the scholarship, his terror of telling *Papá.* But those confessions were far from the worst.

Salva had made his mother all kinds of promises that last day in the hospital. He had sworn never to quit, never to lie. *Never to fail.* If she would *just* get better.

His mother had laughed, even though she hadn't had enough strength in her body to turn over her hand and clasp his own.

And that same night, she had died. As if his promises were worthless.

They had been. He'd broken every one of them. *"Lo siento, Mamá. Lo siento."*

He apologized for letting her down. For being a hypocrite. For claiming he would help *la familia* when all he wanted to do was escape from them.

He didn't bother to wipe away the tears.

There was no point. He had yet to confess about the wall— the barrier he couldn't let go, or rip down, or demolish. Because it was his only defense. Against her.

And the pain. The pain from his mother's last days in the hospital. The winces she had made when she had thought he wasn't looking. And the resignation—that awful resignation he had begged God to remove from her face.

Salva had been so angry. At God. At *Papá* for not taking her to the doctor sooner. At the doctors for failing to save her. And most of all with his mother. For leaving. For her denials those final months, claiming that nothing was wrong; her refusals to seek help; her hushed arguments with *Papá* about the cost.

But it was Salva who had committed the ultimate betrayal. "*Lo siento, Mamá,*" he apologized. For refusing to think about her.

Or remember her.

Or say good-bye.

Arms pulled him from the darkness. Gently. Then Beth's voice. Unbroken. "Tell me about her."

He couldn't answer.

The arms around him tightened. "Please."

Why was she asking this of him? Why did she *keep* asking? Beth didn't need to know about death. She already knew. She had written about it.

But then he realized she hadn't meant death. "Tell me about *her,*" she had said.

And this time he peeled past the anger and the pain. To find . . .

A song—the memory of his mother in church, her voice raised in melody, lyrics spilling from her throat, even though she couldn't read the hymnals. "She liked to sing," he whispered. Suddenly, he could see her in the fields, tilting her head back and singing beneath the sun. And in the garden, singing while pulling dandelions and buttonweeds. He could see her in the flower beds as she planted the lilies.

"She could make anything grow," he murmured, "especially her flowers."

Beth dropped her embrace and crossed her legs on the grass. "Her flowers?"

"*Azucena.*" He reached toward the etchings in the tombstone. "They're white lilies." The stone was cold. He jerked away, trying not to think how the real flowers by the single wide had turned brown and sickly after his mother's death.

Beth covered his hand with her own. "What else?"

His heart scrambled for more details—for a way to explain who his mother had really been. "She could fix things," he blurted.

"What things?"

The kitchen sink: his mother had unclogged the pipes. And the bathroom cupboard: she had sanded the paint on the cupboard door so it would close. But those weren't the type of things Salva had meant. "People," he whispered, thinking of the time Lucia had cried after getting her wisdom teeth pulled. And when Miguel had had to give up the stray dog that had followed him home. And whenever Salva had been afraid, his mother had always been there.

"She just . . ." He closed his eyes and remembered. She had never tried to tell him what to do. Had never pushed. Or let him escape his own responsibilities for making a decision. "She knew how to listen."

Fingers threaded through his own.

Beth wasn't like his mother, Salva thought. Beth *always* pushed.

But as he opened his mouth to describe *Mamá's* patience, the words died on his lips. Because when it came to the important things—to her children's future—*Mamá* had been *less* than patient. She was the reason they were all here—Miguel, Lucia, Salva, Talia, and Casandra. And *Mamá* was the one who had made *Papá* promise that all her children would get an education.

She would have taken Beth's side of the scholarship argument. Would have expected her son to have the strength to tell his father the truth. *Hijo*, she had always said, *you have to make your own choices.*

Dusk had arrived by the time Salva opened the green door and entered the Shrine. His father was waiting, facing the altar. The girls were nowhere in sight. Lucia must have taken Talia and Casandra to the celebration. Salva knew the mariachi band had arrived downtown. Every note and word of "Cielito Lindo" could be heard clearly, echoing down the streets.

He shut out the music, then faced the photo above the mantel. For the first time in four years, he allowed himself to seek help in his mother's eyes. *"Papá,"* he said, "I can't take that scholarship."

His father didn't even turn. "It's that girl, isn't it?"

What? And then Salva remembered the kiss in the street.

"These privileged girls"—Señor Resendez removed a spent candle from its holder—"they don't know what hard work is."

Privileged?

"They mess with your mind," *Papá* continued, "wreck your life, then blame you for their problems."

Salva had known his announcement wouldn't go over well. But these accusations?

Papá was *so* off base.

"Beth isn't like that." Salva banged his shoulder on a lampshade, knocking the tin object to the floor.

Now his father turned, the candle still in his hand. "Did she celebrate your scholarship?"

Dammit. This conversation wasn't supposed to be about Beth. "I don't want to be an engineer."

"Saturday you reach your dream, and now she pulls you down. That's how these girls work, Salva."

Papá had no right—none—to say that. Mr. Take-That-Plate-to-Charla. "You want everything your way." Salva crossed the room to the central barrier of a cedar chest. "You want me to grow up and get an American education and an American job, but raise a nice Mexican family with Mexican values and Mexican children. You can't have it both ways! I'm an American. I've lived here half my life. I want more! I want to study the subjects I'm interested in! I want a career that means something! I want to date the person who understands that!"

"There are plenty of nice girls—"

"Like Char? She's sleeping with Pepe." It was a major betrayal, but Salva had had enough.

For once his father didn't have a response.

"Beth is different! She's so smart she's going to Stanford, and she wouldn't blow that on me if I crawled across the floor and begged her. She's been tutoring me all year in AP English, and if I get the valedictorian slot, she's the reason."

"And what good is that?" His father clenched his hand, crushing the candle stub. "If you throw it away?"

"I'm going to college!" Salva yelled at the top of his lungs. "I'm just not going to be an engineer."

"You can't afford to throw away an opportunity like that."

Of course. Of course that was what his father would say. Salva buried his head in his hands. Maybe this was the problem with having parents who wanted you to do better than they had. You weren't satisfied with what they wanted. He released his head and looked back at the portrait, then at his father. Salva lowered his voice. "I'm not going to wind up working at the onion plant, *Papá.* That's what you're afraid of, isn't it? That I'll spend my entire life like you working for someone else. But I won't."

His father tossed the candle into the trash can beside the fake hearth. "You change your mind in one week. You're too young to know what you want."

"I can't lock myself into a career that means nothing to me."

"How do you know it has no meaning if you haven't tried it?"

Salva stepped back to retrieve the fallen lampshade. It refused to reattach. He gave up and tossed it onto the couch. Might as well admit the entire truth now, though he knew his father didn't trust anything having to do with the government. "I think . . ." he stuttered, "I think maybe I'm going to study law."

Papá's hand closed on the rosary beads on the altar. "Why would you want to do that?"

"Because I'm not like you. I can't just ignore the world around me." Salva hadn't meant the words to come out as an accusation, but they did. "I can't stay silent in the line at the grocery store while people gripe about the language I'm speaking or tell me how worthless the immigrants who work for them are. I can't watch my coworkers being rounded up or see the people I love jump every time the phone rings."

A brittle edge entered his father's voice. "You think it would be better if I argued with *la migra* and convinced them to throw me in jail? So that my family goes hungry while *la policía* decide whether or not to deport me?"

"They can't—"

"They can do anything, Salva." The beads rattled. "If not to me, then to someone else. You know what happens if I lose my job for arguing with the police? Then the people who work under me, like Señora Mendoza, get deported because they don't have the correct paperwork. You think it's easy? Doing nothing. But sometimes that's the only way to protect the people around you, especially the ones you care about."

"Is that what you want from me?" Salva gripped the barren lamp stand. Hard. He couldn't do nothing—couldn't live by that mantra. If that was the way the world worked, he couldn't live with it. "You want me to live here in this culture, in this country, seeing the people I grew up with maligned, and say nothing? So I can benefit from the citizenship you earned me. Until when? Until I forget where I'm from? Or everything you and *Mamá* and Lucia and Miguel did for me? Because that's what would happen. That's what would happen if I took a job I didn't care anything about except for being successful. I can't do that, *Papá*! I'm not you!" The Shrine blurred before his eyes, and Salva whirled.

Then slammed his way out of the house.

21

GASOLINE

Beth was lost, amid the throbbing pulse that was Cinco de Mayo: the racing guitars and high dancing trumpets of the mariachi band; the vibrant reds, greens, blues, and yellows of the swirling folk dancers; the steaming aromas of everything from shredded pork to chicken fajitas to teriyaki shish kabobs. The streetlights gleamed overhead, holding the night at bay.

She closed her mouth on her straw and inhaled a long sip of blueberry lemonade.

The prospect of trying to find Ni in this crowd was overwhelming.

Everywhere there were lines: at the dunk tank, shooting stalls, baseball targets, even to throw Ping-Pong balls at the jars of goldfish. And all the lines merged, bumping and twining their way into the center of Main Street, where they had to compete with the picnic tables, benches, lawn chairs, and undefined dance space.

A little girl in a spray-painted cowboy hat trekked up to Beth. "Can you fix my shoe?" she asked, holding out a small leather-encased foot, barely visible beneath the hulking pink teddy in the child's arms. Beth bent down and closed the Velcro strip. "Better?"

A candy-smeared grin offered up thanks.

"Mari, what are you doing? Come on!" A husky woman toting a diaper bag yanked the girl away.

Beth watched them go, then returned her gaze to the perimeter of the street. *Somewhere there has to be a giant strawberry.*

The mariachi trumpets wailed the final notes of their current number, and a whoop went up from the crowd.

There! Across from the dance space.

Boom! A paper firecracker landed at Beth's feet. She jumped, clapping her hand to the top of her drink. The lid stayed on. A gang of unfamiliar tweens laughed nearby. Beth skirted around them. The aura of the night was far too spectacular to waste her energy scolding. And besides, she had seen the strawberry.

Moments later, she reached the shortcake booth, a wide rectangular stall with an eager throng enveloping three of the four sides. Beth circled around, forcing herself to look at faces rather than the enticing servings of berries and cream. *No Ni.* The plan had been to meet here. At five thirty P.M.

Beth knew she was beyond late.

Salva had needed her.

Nalani could be anywhere. There was really no point in continuing the search.

A trio of young girls waltzed by bearing bowls of the delectable dessert. Beth joined a line.

The band had picked up again, strings and brass flirting with syncopation. Two more songs passed as she waited, sipping her drink slowly. She adored flavored lemonade.

And shortcake. She reached the side of the booth. A man in a red apron lifted a ladle and drenched a rectangle of vanilla cake in thick syrupy berries, then sprayed the top with swirling mountains of whipped cream. Beth devoured the view. She swept the last of her summer money onto the outstretched counter. And accepted the mouthwatering confection. Then she grabbed a fork, ducked under the counter, zipped her way to the corner of the stall, and escaped the shortcake crowd.

To crash right into Salva.

Whipped cream everywhere! He was drenched in lemonade. There were cake and berries on his shirt; syrup dripping down his arms. The bowl and cup at his feet. His face was turning purple.

"Oh, I didn't mean . . ." She spun to the counter and hunted for a napkin, snagged a wrinkled one, and whirled back. "I'm sorry."

"Sorry?" A strange note tinged his voice as he flicked berries from his shirt.

"I'm so sorry!" She tried to wipe syrup off his skin.

He jerked away. "For this?" Still that strange tone. "You're sorry for *this*?"

What did that mean?

"*This* is nothing." He turned away from her and started back into the crowd.

If it was nothing, then why was he leaving? And why was he here? When they'd left the cemetery, she'd asked if he wanted to come to the celebration, and he'd said no—that he needed to talk with his father.

She hurried after him. "Salva?"

He ignored her, pulling ahead and blitzing his way across the street. Not stopping. Not pausing for anyone. He thwacked a kid with his elbow and didn't even apologize. Just kept walking.

Something is wrong, Beth thought as she tried to keep up.

He shoved his way past benches, barking dogs, and another batch of kids throwing noisemakers. Just when she thought she would never catch him, a screaming firework spun into the rare stretch of open pavement in front of his feet. He jumped away, and the screamer exploded in a harsh flare of white light.

She hurried to his side. The firework had gone out. Whoever had set it off had split. "Are you hurt?" she asked.

He shook his head, his eyes closed, his chest heaving.

She reached for him, but he rejected her touch.

"Then what is it?" she questioned. "I thought you weren't coming tonight. That you and your father were going to talk."

Salva's eyes flew open. "We talked!" He gestured abruptly at the shirt covered in strawberry stains. "And unlike this, that disaster is not exactly going to wash out!"

What had happened? If she could just understand—

"It was awful, all right?!" His hands clenched his head. "It was all about you."

What? What had been about her? The discussion with his father? But—

He kicked a charred remnant of the firework. "I told him I wanted to reject the scholarship."

"You . . . you did?"

"And you know what, Beth? It wasn't okay. I knew it wasn't going to be okay!" The night began to implode around her. Had she been wrong to try to talk Salva out of the scholarship? There was a whole side to him that she didn't know—his family, the side of him that had never let her in. But his father cared—she knew that much.

Unlike her mother. Beth had tried, and failed, to explain that difference earlier. That despite the fact that her mother had made an effort recently to keep the fridge stocked and attend her AA meetings, sooner or later she was bound to implode. And Beth hadn't been willing to risk her relationship with Salva on someone that dubious.

But Señor Resendez loved his son.

And Salva was so brilliant. Plus, it was the *wrong* scholarship. "Salva, you're so gifted—"

"Oh, shut up, Beth!" His words slammed into her stomach. "Life isn't a dream."

She reeled backward. She *had* been dreaming. All month.

He kept talking. "It doesn't matter if we're gifted. We're still just two kids from the backside of nowhere."

She reached for him again, unable to help it.

He flung her hands away. "We might as well face it, Beth. This isn't going to last. None of it is going to last!" The trumpets were screeching. She felt like she'd stepped into their blare. The smell of the street had switched to smoke, and her pulse pounded beneath her temples.

His eyes had darkened. He shook as he continued: "We might as well end it now."

What? Was he breaking up with her? *This afternoon he trusted you,* the voice in the back of her mind argued. But it didn't matter. None of it mattered.

The music had died.

"Hey, Resendez!" A familiar shout broke through the lull. "You wanta blow this joint?"

Salva's head turned.

A flash of silver ripped through the air. And he caught the blur. *Keys.*

He started to leave. She had always known he would leave. Since September. But that hadn't stopped her. Had never stopped her from falling in love with him.

Why did she have to accept this now? When she had lost the ability to move. Or breathe.

He'd reached the cones that divided the street from the side traffic.

And there, just outside the cones, sat Pepe Real in his yellow convertible. One arm raised over the front passenger's-side door in a parting salute toward a blond woman who stood in a food line. His mother, gesturing at her son to move into the driver's seat. He just waved her off.

Salva reached the vehicle.

Wait! Beth wanted to shout, but fear had drowned her voice. What would she do if he did stop? Would she run? Plead? Rip the keys from his hand and fight?

He slid behind the wheel.

Tell him she loved him?

The door slammed. And without a backward glance, he drove away.

Headlights swept around the car, burning into the darkness. Salva couldn't see. Anger seared the backs of his eyeballs, his mind, all the way into his skull. It had to be past one A.M., but there were still too many *friggin'* people on the highway.

Honk!

"Yeah, f-you!" Pepe shouted out into the night from the direction of the passenger's seat.

The air blasted through the windows. Cold. Salva wanted the cold. Anything to numb the anger.

It hadn't worked—the night, the car, the speed. He still couldn't annihilate the memories of earlier that evening. He had maligned his father. Broken *Papá*'s dream into pieces, then attacked him as if the loss was his fault. Disrespected the one person who had believed in him longer than anyone else.

Another set of headlights blitzed by.

Salva was the one who had failed. Failed to earn enough scholarship money to go where he wanted to go and study what he wanted to study. Why couldn't he just be happy with what he'd earned?

Honk!

The car swerved. "Relax," Pepe said.

Salva couldn't relax—couldn't come even close to relaxing.

He found himself fighting, over and over again the same arguments. With himself. With his father. With Beth. Salva cringed at the memory of her wounded expression. It had sliced into him. Why? *Why* had she been the one to step right into his path when he'd needed to explode? She wasn't like other people. She didn't just brush off insults. He *knew* that. The walking disaster area? He was the disaster. Stomping on everyone he loved as if they were waiting to be crushed.

Honk!

"Christ!" Pepe shouted. "Just pass this guy, okay?"

Another set of headlights blew around the convertible.

Why didn't I tell Papá earlier about Beth? Salva knew the answer. He was a coward. She had been right about that. He should have told his father the truth. Should have reintroduced Beth to *Papá* weeks ago. *Should have listened to my damn older sister.*

His father thought Beth was privileged. The comment hadn't made any sense at first. But Salva got it now. *Papá* didn't know her. He'd seen her in the Cell, and then she'd shown up at his door the same afternoon. As if she hadn't faced any consequences. And Beth had been wearing that dress. That fancy white dress.

Again the car swerved.

It's my fault. My fault I want what I don't deserve. That I hurt everyone—

Bang! Something plowed into the car. He felt the impact in his entire body. They were spinning. Spinning out of control. Everything was a blur. Panic slammed up to his throat.

His head hit the door. He couldn't defend himself.

The car was still spinning. No sense of friction. Or traction. Only absence.

Salva slid, and his thigh rammed into a barrier. What the hell had happened to his seat belt?

Bang! Steel crumpled like aluminum.

And then the pain. There was nothing but pain. No longer any movement. Or sound. Or color. Except the blinding white, red, black splintering pain. At first it was everywhere. His head, his chest. His leg—his leg didn't feel like a leg anymore. He reached for his thigh, the shattering torn center of agony. And felt bone. *Shit!* And blood. His hands were covered in blood.

He still couldn't see. Everything was dark. He raised his arm to his head. *More blood.*

Someone was screaming.

I should help. He reached for the door, trying to detach his mind from the agony. From himself. His hand slid off the latch. And then he couldn't find it. Couldn't sense anything but the pain.

More screaming.

And then the smell of gasoline.

Out. We have to get out.

He scrambled again for the latch. And the door opened. It was a miracle the door opened. The night rushed in. With even stronger fumes of gasoline.

Oh God, we have to get out of here.

Screaming.

He tried to move.

And realized the scream was his own.

22

TRAUMA

The phone rang, somewhere beyond the grim darkness of Beth's bedroom.

She rolled, burying her tearstained face in her mattress. *Just two kids from the backside of nowhere,* Salva had said. And that was true. What had made her think she had a right to critique his path for escape?

A second ring.

He had gotten what he thought he wanted, and she had waged her disapproval against him. Because *she* had thought he should want more. A regular Lady Macbeth.

A third ring. *Why* was someone calling? The person on the other end should have figured out by now that anyone sane would be asleep at this hour, leaving only the insane.

Beth covered her ears with her hands. She had flung her pillow against a wall ages ago, then never bothered to retrieve any of the blankets tangled in a heap on the floor. Or to change her clothes.

Riiing!

Perhaps it was actually morning and the darkness that saturated her room was only a reflection of her own devastation. She stretched a hand toward her nightstand and shifted her alarm clock, then squinted at the red characters: 2:20 A.M.

Riii—

"Yes?" Her mother's voice was rife with anger. *When had she come home?* A lamp flicked on in the main room, the periphery of light piercing the bedroom's shadows. Beth's body tensed, prepared for her mother to yell, but instead the voice softened. "Who?" A pause. "Yes, but she's asleep. I can tell her in the morning."

Tell me what?

"Oh, you think so?" The voice drifted away. "I don't know, Keala . . ."

Ni's mother? Beth sat up. Too fast. Her head spun. Had something happened to Ni? Why else would Mrs. Villetti be calling at this hour?

Beth scrambled to her feet, then staggered out into the space with the light.

Ms. Courant looked up from the phone. She seemed to wince. "I'll ask," she said. And hung up.

For a moment, silence stretched.

Beth's stomach churned with fear. "Is Ni all right?"

"Ni is fine." Her mother's expression held no comfort. "But she received a disturbing phone call about a car accident tonight involving someone named . . . Salva?"

No.

Beth backed away from the light.

"Mrs. Villetti says she and Nalani are going to the hospital."

Hospital? An image of blood streamed into consciousness.

"They're coming by here in five minutes, if you want to . . ."

Beth spun back to her room. *Her shoes; where were they?* She began picking up bedcovers and hurling them onto the mattress.

The light flicked on above her.

"They aren't releasing details yet," her mother's voice continued, "but at least one of the accident victims is in critical condition."

Critical was serious. Critical was how the doctors had referred to Grandma before she had died.

Beth dropped to her knees and looked under the bed. There were the shoes.

She jerked up, hitting her head on the metal frame. *Dear God, please let him live.* She dragged the shoes out and shoved her feet into them.

"Beth . . ." Her mother blocked the doorway. "There was also a fatality."

God, no. Please!

Beth tried to force her way around the barricade. A hand gripped her arm. "Who is this boy?"

He can't be dead. He can't!

At that moment headlights pierced the trailer.

Beth tore out of her mother's grasp and plunged past.

But the screen door refused to open. The harder she pulled, the more the nightmare closed around her. She pounded the screen, then kicked it.

"Calm down."

Calm down? He could be dead. He could be dead. No! Don't think that. If you think that, you might make it happen.

Her mother reached for the latch and opened the door.

The Villettis' Blazer had turned around and pulled up to the curb, the engine still running. Beth raced to the vehicle and climbed in the back. Ni switched positions to sit beside her.

"Buckle up," Mrs. Villetti demanded.

Beth's fingers wouldn't work. Her friend attached the buckle. *Click.* It was twenty minutes to the nearest town with a hospital.

"Luka called," Ni said. "The team has a phone tree. Pepe's convertible—I guess it's totaled. Apparently, there were three vehicles involved, but according to the hospital, the people in the truck and other car only had moderate injuries."

Which left Pepe. Pepe or Salva.

Please, God, please. Please don't let Salva be dead. He deserves to live.

It was a selfish, horrible prayer. Of course Pepe deserved to live, too, but Beth couldn't spare her heart for him.

We might as well end it, Salva had said.

It could *not* end like this. Those could not be the final words she ever heard from him.

This was her fault. He had argued with his father because

of her. Had left Main Street because of her. Had gotten in that car—that beautiful sleek yellow car—because he had been angry at her.

"We'll get through this," Nalani said. "We'll get through this together."

But this wasn't the kind of thing Beth could get through. Death wasn't like that. Death took. It emptied your reality, sucking the love out of your world. And left you alone.

Were these the last minutes in which she could believe that Salva was alive? A cry escaped from her chest. She could not let him be dead. People weren't meant to disappear from your life without time for you to plan or prepare or realize that no matter how much time you had to prepare it was never going to be enough. *Dear God, let him live.* Every feeling, every image, every memory she had of him wanted to rush into her brain and feed her plea. He was the boy who had listened when she talked about her grandmother. The one who said "please" when he asked for help. The one who had cried in Beth's arms. The boy *everyone* followed.

Salva was immortal. He couldn't be dead. He couldn't.

Unless she had broken him.

Unless she had made him breakable.

The hospital lights scalded Beth's brain. Cops, four of them, lined the entrance. *They could tell me,* she thought as she walked through the aisle of black uniforms. *They could tell me if he is alive.*

Mrs. Villetti hurried her forward. "Girls, you go to the

waiting room," she said, pointing to a sign down the hall. "I'll ask for information at the front window."

Beth's gaze shot to the man behind the lined glass. *He knows. He has to know.*

Ni took her best friend's arm and pulled her down the hall, toward a sign.

Beth halted before reaching it. There were voices coming from the waiting room—voices in Spanish wrenched with sobs.

Beth could no longer walk.

Ni's fingers tightened on her friend's arm and pulled her through the doorway.

The sobs grew louder. A Latina woman huddled in the corner, her torso bent, grief shattering her bowed figure. A younger woman had her arms wrapped around the first, dark hair obscuring half her own face.

But that face was familiar. *Salva's older sister.*

Beth's body went numb.

Along the wall stood Mr. Resendez. Stiff. And stalwart. There were no tears on his cheeks.

"Beth." A hand closed on her shoulder.

She jumped, fear ripping through her chest.

Luka stood beside her. "It wasn't him," he said, shaking his head. "It was Char."

Char?

"There were three of them in the convertible. Pepe, Salva, and Char. The guys are in critical—"

Then a wild scream came from the hall, the female voice shredding Beth's fragile soul.

"No!" Pepe's mother tore into the waiting room, her blond hair in disarray, her body vibrating. A man in a nurse's uniform followed. He tried to pull her back, but she yanked away, screaming again, this time right at Salva's father. "I'll press charges! Your son killed *my* boy! Her daughter"—she pointed at the sobbing woman—"and my son! If Salva ever comes out of that ER, I'll see he's convicted of manslaughter!"

Mr. Resendez didn't move. Didn't argue. Didn't try to apologize.

"Ma'am, please!" The nurse was begging. "These people are all suffering."

But Beth didn't hear what else was said. She lost her balance and sank, her back against the wall, to the floor. Her entire body began to shake as she closed her eyes.

Salva was alive.

23

ETERNITY

Time had no meaning. Beth's inner clock noted only the entrances and exits of the people in the waiting room. Pepe's mother had gone, leaving the implications of her tirade. Mrs. Villetti entered to confirm that Salva's condition was critical. Char's mother departed, her trembling form sheltered by the protective arm of Lucia, who went with her.

Then Tosa arrived, sinking to the floor at Beth's side, his eyes rimmed in red, his arms limp, his face drawn. He looked exactly as Beth felt.

"Did . . . did you see them tonight?" she managed.

He groaned, raising his hands to the sides of his head. "Babysitting. Didn't see any of them." He slumped farther down. "My mother calls that luck." His reddened gaze looked into Beth's, and she knew neither of them felt any gratitude for not being in that car.

After that, there was only silence between them.

He disappeared without her even noting his exit.

Her mind swam with grim questions. Had Salva's spine been shattered? Were his organs shutting down? Was he brain-dead?

A hand gently shook her shoulder. "It's time to go home," said Mrs. Villetti. "You need sleep."

Sleep? Beth stood but only to sink onto a hard bench. She couldn't sleep. If she did, she might wake to find Salva dead. Beth leaned her head against the wall and let Mrs. Villetti's words roll past her.

At last the woman gave up, departing with her daughter and Luka.

Which left only the stiff, silent figure of Mr. Resendez, across the room. But Beth clung to the presence of the man who hated her. As long as he was here, she knew Salva was alive.

Strangers drifted in, no doubt with their own tragedies and concerns. They stood. They paced. They left.

Then another group of strangers. And another.

Eventually, Lucia returned. She also sat across the room, next to her father, a Bible gripped in her hands. Her lips moved, reading out loud.

Beth closed her eyes and began her own hundredth prayer.

Which her mother annihilated.

"Beth Courant!" The woman swept into the room, the ties of her shapeless cleaning uniform hanging loose, the collar flipped in the wrong direction. "It's seven A.M." Her eyes pinned her daughter's, and her feet closed the gap. Then she seemed to take in the fact that she had an audience. *Every* set of eyes in the room was watching. Even Mr. Resendez's hazy stare. Ms. Courant lowered her voice. "Have you eaten anything?"

Beth hadn't even thought about hunger.

Her mother's voice rose. "You know I can't afford to have you end up as a patient at this hospital."

You think this is about money? Beth tugged her legs up on the bench and wrapped her arms around her knees.

"Young lady, I have work in less than an hour."

So go to work.

"I am not your own personal taxi service."

Oh, so now you think this is about your schedule? Beth hugged her knees tighter.

"You get up and get in that car!"

Beth wasn't moving.

Her mother's eyes flew toward the exit, then back. "I don't even know who this boy—"

"I'm staying."

Her mother reached for Beth's wrist. "I do not have time for this. You're getting in that car if I have to pull one of the cops from the entrance to drag you out!"

Beth stood. If her mother was determined to have this argument, they would have it. "You want to know who Salva is?!" She shook off her mother's grip. "He's the one person who's been there for me all year, when Ni was too busy with her boyfriend and you were out at your meetings or taking classes or cleaning the hotel all week so you could come back and bitch about how worthless I am. *He's* the one who actually thinks I'm worth something. Who cares about what I want. Who thinks I deserve to go to Stanford. Who listens!" Emotion pulsed through Beth's body at the chance of release. "So if you want to yell at me, that's fine. But I'm not leaving until I know he's all right!"

Her mother backed away, turned, and stumbled around a man in the doorway as she exited from the room.

A man in a long white doctor's coat.

He stepped toward Salva's father, who was still staring, eyebrows furrowed, at Beth.

"Mr. Resendez"—the doctor's tone was solemn—"I need to speak with you."

24

SILENCE

The screaming in the convertible didn't stop. Salva's own voice had relinquished its volume, but his ears still rang with a scream. Pepe's, he realized.

He called out his best friend's name.

Only the scream. No other response.

And Char? Why couldn't he hear Char?

We still have to get out, *Salva thought. The pain didn't matter.* He had to get out of this car before the gasoline . . .

Salva knew he couldn't put any pressure on his leg. There was just no way. But the door was open, and he didn't have to climb to get to the ground. If he could just get past the pain.

The scream grew louder.

And that was enough. The voice. The agony.

Salva forced himself to fall.

There was nothing after that. Only the shrill fire of sensation. He had no idea how long he lay there. Before he saw the body.

A shadow. But he knew it was Char. Had to be. She must have been thrown from the vehicle.

She wasn't screaming.

The pain that had made it impossible to move before now became nothing, a separate entity blocked off. She was fewer than six feet away. He could make that. He could crawl.

Using only his arms, he pulled himself up toward her legs. They didn't even look injured. But she wasn't moving.

He hauled himself toward her chest.

Still no movement. His eyes had adjusted to the dark, and he could see the insignia on her T-shirt, but no blood.

Again he hauled himself forward.

Her face—there wasn't any blood on her face either. Maybe she was just unconscious. He propped himself on one of his elbows, then reached to touch her throat. Couldn't find her pulse. Or hear her breath. But that didn't mean anything. He'd barely been able to feel the door latch when he'd pulled it. His fingers slid to her cheeks and around her ears, across her hair. To the back of her head.

And then he knew. He knew she was dead.

Because he was holding her brain in his hands.

Salva woke to the headlights, burning his eyes. He flinched, and felt his mind explode. An electronic noise pulsed within his brain. *Beep, beep, beep.* It clashed with the screaming—the screams that had been Pepe's. Until they had stopped.

The lights withdrew, turning to a single tiny bulb. Then a stranger's voice. "Can you tell me your name?"

What a stupid question. Salva groaned. His scalded eyes took in a long silver stand, with tubes. The hospital. *Not this nightmare as well.*

A figure in a white coat was leaning over him. "Salvador, can you squeeze my hand?"

Another stupid question. It was his leg that felt like shit.

He closed his eyes, prepared for the accident to return.

Beep. Beep. Beep. The noise refused to stop, like an ambulance backing up. He didn't want it. Didn't want that sound.

A second voice. "Salvador, can you tell me what year it is?"

The end. Of everything.

"I need you to respond."

He didn't want to respond—didn't have the right. He belonged in the nightmare. But the voices sliced over him.

"I don't know. There was nothing in the CT, but I don't like that he's not talking."

"You wouldn't be talking either if you were on the drugs he's on."

"You don't think we should wait?"

"How long? That leg is messed up."

"I don't like to put him under if he was out for concussion."

"Not concussion. Shock. His pressure was trashed. The kid is strong. I still can't believe he was out of that car."

"I don't want to take him into surgery if—"

Surgery? The word ripped through Salva's charred brain. They thought they were going to fix him? He didn't deserve to be fixed.

His eyes closed, and he returned to the convertible.

The darkness locked him in. He could hear the screams, feel the blood. His hand slipped off the door latch again. Trapped.

His father's voice interfered, a cascade of Spanish. *"Por favor, dame tu perdón."*

Why would *Papá* need forgiveness? Salva rolled his head away.

"He will not talk to me." The voice switched to English. "We had a fight." *A fight?* That had come before Salva had forfeited the right to speak. *Papá* continued, "Maybe his sister."

Don't—

They let in Lucia. Her voice flowed past Salva, around him, beyond.

Again he fell into the crash. In the dark. With the scream. Reaching for the door.

"Beth."

The name severed the sequence.

"She's his girlfriend," Lucia was saying. "Maybe if she came in—"

No! Not *her*. Of all people, Salva could never see Beth again. He forced out the word. "No."

"That's it," said one of the voices. "Prep him for surgery."

Night had fallen by the time Beth returned to the trailer. Ni had come for her and driven her home, though neither of them had much to say. Beth still didn't know any details. The doctors spoke only to family, but Salva had been moved to intensive care. Which meant she had had to leave the hospital overnight.

251

His status had been upgraded from critical to guarded, and that news would have to carry her.

She opened the screen door. To darkness.

"Sit down." The voice came from the shadows.

As her eyes adjusted, they took in a still figure on the far end of the couch. The telling sound of ice clinked against glass.

Stiffly, Beth moved to the empty end and sat.

The shape of a scotch glass lifted from the edge of the couch to Ms. Courant's lips. "I spoke with your teacher, Ms. Mercy, today."

Who? Then Beth realized her mother meant the Mercenary.

Again the ice clinked. "She called to ask about you."

A chill ran along Beth's shoulders.

"She says this young man, Salvador, is quite extraordinary." The ice began to rattle. "Almost worthy of dating my daughter."

What?

"Apparently, Ms. Mercy feels you are the most exceptional student she has ever taught."

Why are you doing this?

"She says this Salvador is taking the hardest classes at Liberty. That he is first in line to become valedictorian. And that everyone in the school is aware of how much he cares about you." The rattling of the ice continued. "I guess if the entire school knows about your relationship, and I don't, then . . . that must be my fault." Ms. Courant offered her daughter the scotch glass.

And Beth took it, desperate to stop the rattling. She sniffed the remnants of the liquid. *Nothing.*

Her mother's voice shook. "I know I haven't been home much

this year. That we haven't . . . I haven't been here for you. And I'd like to claim it's because I was trying to pull things together, but the truth is . . . you've always done so well without me, I didn't want to mess that up."

Beth took a sip from the glass. *Water?*

Her mother sighed. "My father told me a long time ago that I would never amount to anything, and I seem to have proven him right."

Another swallow. It was *really* water.

A trembling hand stretched across the open space on the couch, then pulled back. "I should have told you," Ms. Courant continued, "how *proud* I am of you. And if I have made you feel worthless, then that is *my* fault. Not yours. You are my *daughter.* You always put your heart into everything you do. You always put others first, and today"—the voice broke—"I should have seen . . . I should have seen that that's what you were doing, but when Mrs. Villetti came over this morning and told me she had left you at the hospital, I was so scared . . . I wanted to hit her. Because how could she leave my daughter alone to deal with something like this? And I knew it was really my fault because *I* should have been the one who was there for you, and I didn't know how to be."

Slowly, ever so slowly, Beth reached across the space and touched her mother's hand. "Mom?"

Her mother engulfed her in a fierce hug. "I love you, honey."

And Beth knew she had meant every word.

25

SPEAK

Salva stared at the graphite sketch, slashed by sunlight, on the hospital room wall. One would think the budget could afford a print by van Gogh. Or Monet. Or someone who at least had the sense to paint flowers in color. For a place where so many people drew their dying breaths.

Though Char hadn't drawn hers here. The girl he'd shared a seat with on the bus when he was eight, the one he'd escorted to school for their first day of junior high, the one he'd spent most of the year ignoring and who'd verbally slapped him upside the head a month ago for underestimating his best friend: she had been dead before she'd ever reached the hospital.

Unlike Pepe. According to the newspaper, he had still been alive until an hour and twenty minutes after his arrival. Sometimes people made the mistake of thinking Pepe's toughness wasn't real—that he just used it for intimidation. But Salva knew better—knew his best friend could take out half an

254

offensive line on his own. Pepe had always been the one with the guts. And he'd proven it. In the end.

The article—the one the cops had given Salva an hour ago when they'd come to interrogate him—had included a photo. Of the convertible. The crushed front passenger's side. It was a miracle Pepe had been able to scream.

Salva had forced himself to read the article and assimilate the other details of the wreck. The truck and trailer they'd been passing that had wound up jackknifed in the middle of the road and taken out a power line. The car that had plowed into the convertible, leaving the driver trapped behind the wheel. Though, apparently, the guy had been able to walk once he'd been carved from his seat.

Unlike Pepe.

The cops had left without their statement. They had claimed they needed one, with Pepe's mother threatening to press charges. But Salva knew better. Silence should be enough to confirm that the whole crash was his fault.

His father entered the room without permission. For the millionth time. Apparently, patients had no rights when it came to *la familia*. Earlier this morning, Talia and Casandra had been allowed in. *Why?!* Salva had wanted to yell. There was nothing for them to see. No one to look up to. He hadn't wanted them here, staring wide-eyed at the brace around his leg as if that were somehow the cause of his dissolution.

They'd announced that Miguel was coming home. Another

why? In some futile attempt to prove that *la familia* still existed? Or because it was now clear which son was the greater failure?

"There was a phone call for you last night," said *Papá*.

And I'm supposed to care? Salva let his father's words run past him. The sketch on the wall seemed to grow uglier as he studied it. There were holes between the slash marks. The petals looked as though they had been severed.

"The man said his committee wants to interview you for a scholarship," *Papá* continued. "Is this possible?"

No. The stems in the drawing had thorns. Sharp. And pointed.

"*Hijo,* answer me."

Sí, Papá. If you give out the orders, everyone will have to obey. Charla will go to college. Pepe will behave. I won't be guilty.

"Your sister told the man we had an emergency, but he said the committee has to make a decision this week."

Go away, Papá.

"Which means you have to call them, *hijo.*" His father held out a scrap of paper with a phone number written on it.

Salva thrust away the number. He didn't deserve a scholarship. He didn't have the right to talk. What was the point of speech if you didn't use it when you should? *I don't deserve to be alive.* When would the doctors and his father and everyone figure that out?

Beth returned to the hospital to learn that Salva had been moved from intensive care to the medical/surgical floor. And that she had been left off the approved-visitors list. No doubt the decision of Mr. Resendez. Her mother had driven her to the hospital and stayed for the first hour, which should have helped. And hadn't. *Salva is healing,* Beth told herself as she waited on the thinly cushioned chair in the waiting room of the medical wing. *That should be enough.* But it wasn't. She couldn't be certain. Couldn't know. Couldn't truly *believe* he would recover until she saw him with her own eyes.

She pulled her knees up toward her chest and buried her face in them. *He's alive. He's alive. He's alive.*

"So . . . you're Beth."

Her eyes flew open, and she looked into the forthright gaze of Salva's older sister. Lucia stood above her, holding out a granola bar.

Beth declined the offer by shaking her head.

The other girl sat down at her side. "Sometimes my brother can be so dense."

What?

Lucia tugged on the wrapper of the granola bar. "Oh, I know you must think I'm a horrible sister, but I don't see why he didn't just introduce you to all of us—after *Papá* got over his temper. But Salva can be such a coward." The wrapper split open. "It's a miracle he ever got up the guts to ask you out. Every other girl he's dated was someone that one of his friends recommended." She peeled down the shimmery paper.

"When he was little," Lucia continued, not pausing long enough to take a bite, "he didn't even have friends because he was so shy. Then after we moved here, Pepe conned him into sneaking a snake into the church. Salva was too scared to refuse. And that's how they got to be close.

"You know he wouldn't even try out for the football team in middle school? He was so sure he wouldn't get picked. Tosa and Pepe had to go to the coach and ask him to invite Salva personally."

"H-he doesn't like losing," Beth whispered.

"No." The other girl's voice dropped. "He's never been good at losing anything."

Like his friends.

"H-how is he?" Beth whispered.

"He has a broken femur. The bone came right through his skin, and he lost a ton of blood; but he went through surgery okay." The granola bar fell idle on Lucia's lap. "His head was also bleeding when he first came in. They couldn't do any tests right away because he was in shock. When they ran the CT, it didn't show anything. The doctors don't think he has brain damage, but he's not . . . talking."

Two figures in dark uniforms tromped past the open door.

"Bastards." Lucia shuddered. "They were in Salva's room this morning, without even asking *Papá*'s permission. Not that *Papá* would talk to them. You'd think the cops would back off after the test came back saying Salva hadn't been drinking."

The sound of the boots faded, leaving Beth in shivers. "Do

you . . . do you believe Pepe's mother will really press charges?"

"Pepe's mother is grieving," Lucia murmured. "The police ought to realize that. My brother is a human being. He made a mistake. And his friends are dead because of it. Isn't that enough punishment for anyone?"

"*Hija.*" Mr. Resendez entered the room and shot a disapproving glare at his daughter and her companion. Then he began to pace, his words rushing into more Spanish.

Beth made herself remain at Lucia's side. It would be wrong to abandon the person who had finally answered her questions.

Though the older girl appeared to be holding her own for a half-dozen exchanges. Then she switched to English. "I don't know, *Papá*. You'll have to ask him."

The response was brusque.

"Well, he won't talk to me either!" she argued.

Her father flung his arms into the air.

"*No sé,*" Lucia replied, glancing over at Beth, then back at her father. And back again. "Why don't you ask *her*?"

Instantly, Beth regretted the decision to stay.

The other girl didn't appear to notice, though her attention now fully centered on Beth. "Do you know where my brother applied to go to college?" she asked.

"Of . . . of course," Beth stammered, then reeled off the names of the in-state colleges.

"And those are all the schools?" Lucia asked. "You're certain? It's not possible he could have applied to more?"

"Lucia!" her father snapped.

"¿*Qué*, *Papá*? Maybe she knows—"

"What could she know?" Mr. Resendez replied.

Beth felt the blood rush to her face. This man had no right to belittle her. Or to keep her from seeing his son. "There were three others," she blurted. "I dared Salva to apply to three other colleges."

Mr. Resendez froze.

"You did?" Lucia was grinning.

Beth dropped her chin, knowing if Salva hadn't told his family, there must have been a reason.

"Where?" the other girl demanded. "Where did he apply?"

The error had already been made. Might as well tell the entire truth. "Harvard, Princeton, and Yale."

"That's it, *Papá*!" Lucia said. "Yale University really wants to interview my brother for a scholarship."

Yale.

Mr. Resendez was staring at Beth. "Why would you do that?" he asked. "Why would you dare him to apply somewhere so far away when you also tell him not to take the scholarship at State?"

"I told him not to *settle* for it," she replied. "Your son is the best student at Liberty High. He's gifted. Brilliant. Any school should be grateful to have him."

There was silence.

At last Mr. Resendez sank down into a chair, his head tilted back, his gaze toward the ceiling. "He has to call the scholarship committee. But he won't. It's like he's . . . broken." The man's hands lifted to cover his face. "I don't know what to say to him. He needs—"

"His mother," Beth whispered.

The hands fell, and the silence was intense.

She bit her lip. "He . . . he said his mother could fix people."

Dark eyes lifted, pain raw within them. "He spoke to you about his mother?" Mr. Resendez's voice cracked.

"He said she loved to sing," Beth whispered.

Silent tears spilled down the man's face.

"*You,*" he said at last, blinking fiercely. "You need to talk to him."

"But *Papá* . . ." Lucia whispered. "Salva said—"

"Exactly." Mr. Resendez rounded on her. "And that's the only thing he has said since the crash." The man turned back to Beth, not giving her the chance to ask questions. "If you could dare my son to apply for this school and persuade him to reject a four-year scholarship to another one, then maybe *you* can get through to him. And convince him to complete this interview."

Beth's heart thundered.

His trembling hand stretched, taking her own. At last the larger meaning came flying into her chest.

He was going to let her see his son.

A knock tapped on the hospital room door, followed by the sound of footsteps.

Not again. Salva nailed his gaze to the graphite flowers.

This time the visitor didn't speak.

There came a soft, very light rustle on the left side of his bed.

And then a hand on the back of his own.

He jerked away. No one had touched him like that since . . . *God, no.* She should not be here!

He tried to order her to get out, but the words stuck at the barrier in his throat.

His eyes dropped, following her fingers as she touched the scrap of paper on the bedside table, the paper with the scholarship phone number. Then she reached again for his hand.

He tried very, very hard to remain stiff. To convince himself that if he didn't respond she would leave.

Like everyone else.

But Beth wasn't everyone.

Her arms came around him.

He couldn't let them—couldn't let her hold him. She would hate him when she knew the truth. But perhaps that would be better. His words broke through the invisible barrier. "It's my fault."

The arms tightened.

"I knew," he said. "I knew, and I didn't—"

Her forehead rested on his shoulder.

"I didn't speak," Salva said. *Didn't she get it?* "I could have stopped her. Char was afraid of losing face. Pepe was trying to impress her. He would have listened to me. Char wouldn't have fought. If I'd just . . ."

Beth pulled Salva even closer.

"*I* was supposed to teach her. It was *my* responsibility, but I quit. I knew"—his voice broke—"I knew she couldn't drive."

A shudder rushed from Beth's body to his. She whispered, "You weren't driving?"

"I should have been!" he shouted. "I should have"—he choked on the words—"I should have"—the tears were falling—"*said* something."

He cried in her arms, the tears turning to sobs. His whole body shook until he could not think anymore. Could only feel the huge hole that had been his friends' place in his heart—the girl who had needed him, whom he had let down, and the guy who had always, *always* been there when Salva needed support. He would never recall his past the same way. His childhood. His life.

It seemed impossible that there was anything left.

But Beth was still holding him. Which made no sense. She must hate him. She, of all people, had to have expected more, but she wasn't asking or denying anything. Or trying to absolve him of the guilt. He wouldn't have wanted her to. Because no matter what happened, he had to live with the choice he had made—to pay the price for saying nothing.

He didn't know how long she held him, her heart beating regularly beneath the soaked cotton of her shirt. *How could she be so calm?* He clung to her for his very soul. Until at last his pulse slowed to match hers.

"I shouldn't have pushed you so hard about the scholarship," she whispered, the fingers of her left hand winding through the fingers of his own. "I should have listened."

No, he wasn't about to shift any of that guilt to her. "I had no right to yell at you," he blurted. "I was wrong. I didn't mean any of what I said that night. I was just afraid . . . of losing you." And of the imminent deadline that had seemed to threaten them both.

Her lips brushed his once, twice, then his forehead, his cheek, his mouth again, each kiss a suture, a thin strand stitching the torn threads of his soul together. "We can't go back," she whispered. "All we can do is speak now." Her voice went soft, so soft for a moment he thought he hadn't heard it, that he had only been reading her actions. But the kisses stopped and those brown eyes held his, this time the words unmistakable. "I love you, Salva."

And he knew she meant it. Because Beth always meant what she said.

He had been terrified of that. Of her demands that he tell the truth, that he live up to her incredible standards. And his. Terrified of how deeply he had fallen, how fast things moved when he was with her, how impossible it had seemed to be without her.

Because she was . . .

So much like him in every way.

She was right, of course. He couldn't remain silent. Silence cost too much. His hands went into her mostly brown, sometimes auburn hair, and he kissed her. Slow. There was no race. No rush. No deadline he had to outrun. "I love you, Beth." He spoke.

TRANSCRIPT OF SCHOLARSHIP INTERVIEW
YALE UNIVERSITY
APPLICANT: SALVADOR RESENDEZ

DR. EISMAN: Is the speakerphone working?

PROF. SCHNITZ: Doesn't seem to be. Call someone in.

TECHNICAL SUPPORT: I'm already here. Let's see. No, the plugs are all set. It should be working.

PROF. SCHNITZ: Well, obviously it's not.

TECHNICAL SUPPORT: Let's see. Um . . . did you remember to type in the ID code?

DR. EISMAN: The what?

TECHNICAL SUPPORT: There. Try again.

DR. EISMAN: Testing speakerphone. Can you hear us, Salvador?

APPLICANT: Salva.

PROF. SCHNITZ: That's better. What did you say?

APPLICANT: People call me Salva. Not Salvador.

DR. EISMAN: Very well, Salva. Can you hear our voices clearly enough?

APPLICANT: Yes, sir. They're faint, but I can understand them.

DR. EISMAN: Good. We shall start by introducing you to everyone on the committee. I am Dr. Eisman. I head up the Financial Aid Department. This is Professor Schnitz. He is the head of Admissions.

PROF. SCHNITZ: Hello, Salva.

DR. EISMAN: And Professor Lang. She is in charge of the Foundation for Minority Students.

PROF. LANG: I am glad we could connect with you, Salva. Could you begin by telling us a little about yourself for the record?

APPLICANT: My name is Salva Resendez. I'm a senior at Liberty High School. I'm not sure what you would like to know.

DR. EISMAN: Well, Salva, we've looked through your application, and it is very impressive, but to be frank, we have a lot of strong applicants. And we can't afford to provide all those students with a full scholarship here. We'd like to know what's not on the application that explains why we should select you. What makes you want to come to Yale?

APPLICANT: Um . . . sir, to be honest, it isn't Yale. It's— *vaya, Papá,* you aren't supposed to be here. No, she's not supposed to be here either—sorry about that. It isn't any particular school. It's . . . I need to go somewhere that will help me make the most difference.

PROF. LANG: Make a difference how, Mr. Resendez?

APPLICANT: Can't that wait? No. Argh! Could you come back in twenty minutes and flush the IV then?

PROF. LANG: Excuse me? We don't seem to have your full attention. Are you not interested in this interview?

APPLICANT: Yes, yes, I'm interested! It's just— I guess nobody told the nurse. She's not the one who usually comes in.

DR. EISMAN: Salva, I think my companions and I are a little confused about your situation. I understand from speaking with your sister that there was some kind of emergency in your family this week.

APPLICANT: Yeah, I'm the emergency.

PROF. LANG: Pardon?

APPLICANT: I was in a car accident.

PROF. LANG: Oh, I'm sorry to hear that. I hope it wasn't serious.

APPLICANT: It was. Listen, could I maybe talk about that? I mean, if you want to know something about me that isn't on my application.

DR. EISMAN: Does this have some impact on your choice to go to Yale?

APPLICANT: Yes. That is—I could explain that, I think. You see, people listen to me. It's strange because I've never been the type of person who wanted to stand out from the crowd. Not like my best friend. He was always saying something, doing something, to get people to notice him. I just wanted to fit in. But I don't.

PROF. SCHNITZ: And why is that?

APPLICANT: I'm not sure. My girlfriend calls it a gift. She says I shouldn't throw it away.

PROF. LANG: Which means—

APPLICANT: And I didn't get it. Not until the crash. I always knew I had to do well in school. It's a big deal to my father. He and *Mamá*—they brought our whole *familia* here to this country, and he's worked really hard to see that my brother, sisters, and I could get an education. Not just a diploma, but college, a good one. I never wanted to disappoint *Papá*. It's just . . . I didn't figure out what it was I wanted to do. Until this week.

PROF. SCHNITZ: And what is it you want to do?

APPLICANT: To speak. For all the people who need it. I used to get so angry at my father because he wouldn't defend himself. He and most of his friends—they don't want to risk questioning people with authority, which leads to some pretty lousy communication. Around here it's usually *los mexicanos* who wind up at the bottom. But it's that way for someone everywhere. And this week I realized it isn't my father's job to speak up; it's mine.

DR. EISMAN: And you came to this realization because of an accident?

APPLICANT: My best friend had this car—sweet—a real operator, kind of like him. He asked me to drive it, but we picked up his girlfriend on our way out of town, and then he offered her the keys. Anything for a little more credit, that was Pepe. But she couldn't drive well. She never took driver's ed because she couldn't apply for a license. With the law now, you have to prove you're a citizen to get one.

DR. EISMAN: We understand.

APPLICANT: But I knew she wasn't a good driver. And I didn't say anything.

PROF. SCHNITZ: About what?

APPLICANT: I didn't tell her not to drive. I didn't tell Pepe not to let her. And they both died. The cops wanted me to make a statement saying the accident wasn't my fault. They said they could tell from forensics. But this isn't about forensics.

I could have stopped the crash. If there was anyone anywhere who could have, it was me. And I didn't do it.

I took the easy way out. Only it wasn't easy. My friends, Pepe and Char, they didn't die easy.

You know what I realized is that leadership isn't some kind of trial to be avoided . . . or endured. It's a responsibility. Like Beth says, a gift.

I want to go into law, maybe politics. I'm smart enough. I can do it. I can tell the truth, and people will listen. So . . . it's not Yale, in particular. Though I think maybe it's the best school on the planet. But what I want—no, what I need—is to go somewhere that's a challenge. Somewhere that forces me to work as hard as I can and learn as much as I can so that, one day, I can maybe make up for saying nothing. I can make that difference for someone else, even if I can't go back and save my friends. You see?

PROF. LANG: Yes, Salva, I believe we see. Thank you for speaking with us today.

APPLICANT: You don't have any other questions?

PROF. SCHNITZ: I think we heard what we needed to hear. We appreciate your being so honest with us.

APPLICANT: Honesty means a lot *en mi familia.*

PROF. SCHNITZ: Yes, I hope we have the honor of meeting them one day.

APPLICANT: I do, too, sir.

DR. EISMAN: Thank you very much.

Epilogue

THE MARCH

"That is the ugliest paint job I have ever seen," Salva couldn't help saying as Beth lifted her plywood sign from the dented-up green pickup bed. WE FEED YOUR FAMILIES, the sign said in red, gold, and purple colors, paint splattered between each word and the next. The reverse side: OUR FAMILIES HAVE RIGHTS TOO had dried drips running from the bottoms of all the letters.

"Yes, well, I guess that's the difference between Yale and Stanford." She pointed at his own sign, resting on top of the high pile still stacked in the back of the pickup. His neat black print spelled out the words IMMIGRANT RIGHTS ARE HUMAN RIGHTS. "Some of us prefer creativity over tradition," she added.

He dropped his crutch against the tailgate, fish-hooked her in his grasp, and pulled her in for a quick kiss, then reached awkwardly to retrieve his own sign from the high pile.

For once he was grateful for the ancient pickup. *Papá* might not be willing to forgo his commitment to his job, but with the provision that Miguel do all the driving, their father had loaned his younger son the transportation for the trip to the city. A good thing, since there had turned out to be a lot more students than Salva had expected, taking up his idea of using Senior Skip Day to attend the regional immigrant rights march. There must have been fifty signs in the pickup bed.

Nalani pulled her parents' Blazer into the next space in the supermarket parking lot. Soon Luka, Tosa, and Linette all bailed out, then rushed over to help unload the plywood signs and canvas banners.

Within minutes the lot was swarming with students from Liberty High, even a few juniors and sophomores, which was sure to drive Markham around the bend. He'd informed Salva that the valedictorian slot could be reassigned if a student was found breaking the law. And Senior Skip Day was against the law.

But Salva really didn't care. Pre-law, he had pointed out, was going to be his focus of study, and he thought he should witness the glory of the First Amendment in action, before he accepted his full ride to Yale University. Valedictorian or not.

Not that Markham was likely to carry out the threat, seeing as how graduation was next week. And the salutatorian was here, too. And almost every senior on the high-school honor roll.

"*¿Dónde vamos, Señor Presidente?*" Tosa draped a banner over the side of the pickup, then took Salva's crutch and slid it inside the emptied bed. "Or are you just taking us to the parking lot? Which way are we headed?"

Salva didn't have a clue. He looked at Beth.

"They start off along Twenty-first Street," she said, propelling herself onto the back of the pickup. "It's just a couple blocks that way." She pointed with her sign.

He grinned. "You see, Tosa, she mocks my organizational skills, but they're already rubbing off on her."

"Yeah, man, and you're losing 'em." Tosa lifted his injured friend up beside Beth. "I don't know what you two are gonna do an entire country apart from each other."

Beth's free hand swept around Salva's waist. "I'd rather be a five-second phone call away anytime," she whispered in his ear, "than lose you." Her gaze was earnest, even in the middle of the chaos around them.

What were a hundred or a thousand or three thousand miles in comparison to the distance between life and death? Salva planted a serious kiss on her.

Whistles followed, along with a dozen mocking comments his best friend would have enjoyed. Salva could picture Pepe, shouting and jumping, pumping up the crowd, thrilled at the prospect of sticking it to the whole frigging establishment.

He was the reason they were here. And Char. Because her life and his were worth something. People should know that.

This wasn't about Salva. He was just the leader.

"Let's go," he said, signaling his peers. "Make a little history for Charla and Pepe! Show people that Liberty is about a heck of a lot more than a football team! What do you say?"

The cheers came in two different languages. Students spread out, some hopping into banner-draped vehicles, motors starting again, and mismatched signs lifting around the parking lot.

Beth's arm tightened on Salva's waist.

He knew there were questions about the future. He might not survive the academic rigors he had chosen. Loss would always underline anything he did achieve. And dreams changed.

But change could be beautiful. His gaze met Beth's, then rose to the flawed sign above her head. Eight months ago he had etched neat perfect outlines to restrain the damage she had done with her painted golden chaos.

When ultimately *he* had been the one who was damaged.

It was her chaos—the glorious unrestrained emotion that was Beth—which had saved him. Her amazing capacity to challenge and love and forgive.

He swept her closer, swapping his own sign with hers. *"Vamos, mi amor,"* he told her.

There was something to be said for paint spattered all outside the lines.

Acknowledgments

Thank you. To my editor, Kristin Gilson, for her insight into this project. To my agent, Kelly Sonnack, for laughing and crying when she read it. To Angelle Pilkington for believing in it first. To Eileen Kreit, Linda McCarthy, Vanessa Han, Pat Shuldiner, Nora Reichard, and the rest of the team from Penguin for helping bring the dream to life. To Tracey, who answered all the obligatory my-sister-is-the-medical-expert-in-the-family questions. To my dad, who walked Tosa through the steps of changing the oil in a car. To Juana Santillan and Yvonne De Los Santos for pinch-hitting my random *preguntas de español.* To Maria Patla and Dawn Sheirbon for their amazing artistry and expertise with my website, school visit brochure, and myriad graphic challenges. To the educators, librarians, fellow writers, bookstore workers, volunteers, and literary supporters who helped make this ultimate dream of being a full-time author come true. And to my readers! Salva would never have learned to speak without *all* of you.